WINDUPBIRD
PUBLISHING

60 Years Later

by
John David California

First published in Great Britain 2009
by Windupbird Publishing Ltd.

ISBN 978-91-85869-54-1

www.windupbirdpublishing.com
www.sixtyyearslater.com

Edited by: Beth Bruno
Structural development: Jaclyn Bond

The author would like to thank the following wonderfullies:
Mother Helena, father Håkan, stepmother Elizabeth, stepfather Gerhard,
big brother Jonas, big little sister Tina, little sister Krystle,
dear friend Carl-Johan, future wife and children.

To J.D. Salinger,

the most terrific liar you ever saw in your life.

1

I open my eyes and, just like that, I'm awake.

J D California

2

I '*m bringing him back. After all these years I've finally
decided to bring him back.*

J D California

3

It feels like I only just closed my eyes but at the same time it feels like I have been sleeping for ages. I stretch my body, take a deep breath, and notice that my back is kind of sore. Maybe I've slept in the wrong position again; it happens to me every so often. Sometimes I wake up in the morning and my arm has fallen asleep, so I pick it up with my other arm and shake it until it comes alive again. It's really a pretty queer feeling, not recognizing your own arm and all.

I think it's because I don't exercise enough. I don't, I really don't. I've never been very athletic but lately it's been even worse. I've mostly been right here, laying in this bed, sleeping or writing or just watching the clouds through the window. But I did quit smoking. I haven't had a cigarette since I came here, so in one way it can't be all bad. At least not when you think of how much I used to smoke just the other week. Anyway, I think this is why my arm falls asleep like that. I should really start exercising.

I can't really say exactly what it is, but there's some kind of foul smell coming from somewhere in the room. Perhaps it's an old sandwich or something I've managed to drop under the bed. I'll have to remember to ask them to look down there when they come to clean later on.

I suppose it's pretty damn early, but it must still be the middle of the night. It's so dark I can hardly see my goddamned hand in front of my face. When I reach out to turn on the light, my hand moves over the top of the table where I put my notebook last night, but I can't find the light switch. I keep searching all around the table and up past my bedpost and back, and I sweep my hand around the entire table again, still without finding it. It's so dark I can't even find my notebook and all I end up doing is knocking something over. I hear it crash to the floor and break into about a million pieces.

Goddamn, I try to say to no one in particular since I have my own room and all, but I only manage a croak. My voice sounds dry and raspy and what I could really use is a cool glass of water. If I could only find the goddamned light switch I could get up without tearing the whole room down.

I feel my bladder like a swollen balloon inside me and I pull the cover down and swing my legs over the edge. There's definitely some foul smell in the room; I can sense it even more now. It's not really a strong odor but it's very present in the way that you can't hide from it no matter which way you turn your head.

The way my back hurts I wonder if something didn't happen to me yesterday. It feels like I've been run over by a train or something, but I can't think of anything out of the ordinary that happened. I was mostly in here, apart from going to the food hall twice, and it was a day just like all the others in this place.

The only thing I can think of that was different about yesterday was that I finished telling you about all this madcap stuff that happened to me lately. I wrote it all down in the notebook, the one I can't even find now because it's so goddamned dark in here.

D.B. drove over last Saturday and even he kept asking me about it, but I didn't know what to say to half of the questions he asked me. I mean, half of the things I do I don't even know why I do. So, I figured, while I still remember most of it, it'd be best if I wrote it down, and I just finished it yesterday. Maybe someday I'll publish it and become famous, just like D.B, but I'll never sell myself to Hollywood like he has, not even if they give me a new car and girl from the movies to go along with it. You gotta have some principles, even when you're famous. You really do.

Perhaps I'm getting the flu or something and that's why I feel heavy all over and my back hurts and all. Now wouldn't that be just perfect. I came here to get well and what happens? I catch the flu. Mom and Dad will have a fit.

I can't believe how awake I feel, even though it's so early. I can usually sleep away half the day and it usually doesn't bother me one bit, but now I feel like I've had enough sleep to last me a lifetime. If I could only find the damn light switch. I really have to get over to the bathroom quickly the way my bladder is killing me.

I stand up and move carefully across the floor with my arms outstretched in front of me. I probably look near right ridiculous, but that would be just like me, walking right into some sharp edge and hurting my leg, on top of it all. I totally forget that I knocked something over and I step right on it and it feels like tiny pebbles of something and they stick to the soles of my feet until I get about an inch taller. I'm lucky it wasn't glass or anything like that. When I get to the wall I have to stop and lift each foot up and scrape whatever it is away.

My body really does feel all weird and heavy;

it's possible it actually could be the flu. I heard them talking the other day of some people on the second floor that had just gotten the flu and had to stay away from the food hall.

I find the door to the bathroom but when I try to step inside I can't because there's so much junk in the way. It's really like a wall of junk that goes all the way from my feet to my head and for about a second I'm really confused. Then, about just as fast, I realize I must have opened the closet door instead. In this damn darkness I could have walked out on the balcony and taken a piss, and I wouldn't have noticed. If I had a balcony that is, which I don't.

I find the right door farther up but then the next strange thing happens. I hope you don't think I'm making this up or anything, I'm really past that, even though I confess that I used to do it all the time before. It's just that everything in the bathroom seems to have switched places during the night. The toilet isn't directly to the left when you go in, like it has always been; instead it's farther up along the wall. What's even more strange is that the shower cabinet has moved from one side of the room to the other and not even in here can I find the goddamned light switch. I must really be getting a bad case of the flu.

I don't even bother looking for the light and I lean against the bowl and feel the porcelain ice cold against my shins as I lean forward and listen to when water hits water. I can't believe how little comes out of me. From the pain in my bladder I would have thought I at least would have carried on for half a minute or so, but it's over so quickly that I almost feel cheated.

I keep my hands outstretched as I move out of the bathroom and into the hallway again. My eyes should really have gotten used to the darkness by now but this isn't like any darkness I've ever seen before. I'm telling you, it's pitch black. The only light I can see in the entire room is a small red dot on the floor under my desk. It looks like it could really be a thousand light years away, floating by itself in all that darkness, and not just a light under my desk.

I'm really thirsty and I don't want to step inside another closet again on my way to the kitchen, so I move my hands along the wall in the hallway until I finally come across the light switch. At first the brightness blinds me and I still can't see a thing, but after a couple of seconds I get used to it and I can finally see the room.

Something must be wrong. I turn the light off and then on again, but it's still wrong. Did they move me while I was sleeping? Because this isn't my room. I mean, I can't recognize a thing in here, not even the room itself.

I'm in some sort of small apartment but it's definitely not the same place I fell asleep in just a few hours ago. This must be a completely different building. Come to think of it, that's actually what it looks like, someone's apartment.

It's so small that I walk around the whole place in just a couple of steps. I go through the hallway where there's a few pairs of shoes on the floor and some jackets and hats on the hat rack, and then when I step into the bedroom I see a really small kitchen to my left, where you couldn't really cook anything even if you wanted to. Then I come to the bedroom itself with a desk and some chairs, a bookshelf and of course the bed.

I stand in the middle of the room and I honestly don't know what to believe. Where am I and how did I end up in this apartment? Perhaps there was a fire and they had to evacuate everyone real quick but I refused to wake up so they just moved me anyway. That's possible, but then where the hell am I?

I go over to the desk and look at the framed pictures standing in a row there. I bend down and look at each one of them closely but they don't give me any clues since I have no idea who the hell the people in them are. As I turn around my foot hits something and I look down. In front of me, on the floor, lays an empty pill bottle and a lots of little pills. It's like a thousand tiny pink little things, all scattered across the floor. So this is what I knocked over before.

It must be that I'm in another wing. The more I think of it the more it makes sense. This place is huge to begin with. I remember it took D.B.'s new girl ages just to go to the ladies room in the other wing. I'm sure it is just something trivial, like a water leak, or a broken window or something, and immediately I start to feel a bit better.

I guess I should hurry and pick these pills up before whoever really lives here comes back and gets all upset and everything. So, I bend down and pick up the empty bottle and, as I do, I catch the name printed on the prescription. It's printed on a paper tag in black block letters and it takes a few seconds for me to realize that it's my own name. But I don't really have time to reflect over it because at the same time I notice my arms.

As I read the text on the jar I see that something is really wrong with my arms. My skin is all prickly and covered with tiny dark spots, almost like freckles, and it's loose and saggy, like my arms have shrunk two sizes during the night and my skin hasn't had time to catch up. The veins on top of my hands are really visible, I mean, they sort of bulge out, and around my knuckles the skin has become wrinkled and scrunched together.

I feel my head begin to spin and I feel really confused. These aren't my arms; these aren't my arms at all. The same way this damn room isn't mine.

I drop the empty bottle back on the floor and hurry to the bathroom. I find the stupid light switch right away this time and I step in front of the mirror. What I see almost makes me fall backwards.

It's not me looking back at me, but an old man. My skin, my hair, my face, my everything is covered in an old man's body. My hair has turned into sort of an electric white and it's become really thin, and my chest looks like it's about to cave in. I can see my ribs and the bones of my shoulders poke out from under my skin. And my skin, my skin has turned into a sagging yellow bag. I look just like a plucked chicken.

For a moment I just stand there and look at the old man looking back at me. He's got sort of a frightened look on his face, but I couldn't care less. I mean, he's the one that has taken over my body, not the other way around. Suddenly the silence has become unbearable. I want to scream to at least hear my own voice. I open my mouth and try but nothing comes out. I push from my stomach until my face gets a reddish tone, or the old face looking back at me in the mirror does, but I can't get a word out. It's like there's a wall in my throat blocking anything from coming out.

I keep my mouth open and I notice that this is where the foul smell is coming from. I've become some sort of monster with rotting flesh and I don't know what the hell to do. Should I call the nurse? I know when she comes she'll get half scared to death and wake up the doctor and I bet in a second all hell will break loose around this place.

My parents will have about a hemorrhage apiece when they find out.

When I think of my parents, suddenly I start to laugh. I know I shouldn't, but it just bubbles up from inside of me and I can't stop it. Somehow the wall is gone and I hear my hoarse and dry laughter echo in the bathroom, and when I do it makes me laugh even harder. I laugh and laugh but now it's not because I think it's funny that my parents will go out of their minds when they get their son back as an old man, or because my voice sounds like a drunken sailor's, but because I realize that this is all a dream.

4

I try to remember when I fell asleep, but I can't remember anything about last night. Well, that's not really true since I still have the same tapping dream that I've had ever since the day I left Pencey a couple of weeks ago, but that's not really something new. But other than that it's totally blank.

About this dream. I think maybe it's because of its nature that I remember it so vividly, but also because of the very simple reason that this is the only dream I have ever had. Of course, I have nothing to compare it to except these weird dreams that Phoebe keeps telling me about, but it's a strange dream all the same. It's not about a person or a place, and it doesn't include pictures or voices of any kind. It's a dream about a sound, a simple tapping sound, like that of an old-fashioned typewriter being punched.

This is so wild, that I'm still sleeping and I know about it at the same time it's happening!

I can't wait to tell D.B. about this, or Phoebe for that matter, but I bet you a dollar they won't believe a word I say. I think there's even a name for this, you know, when you actually know you are dreaming while *in your dream*, but I can't think of it right now.

I look at the old man in the mirror and it feels like I'm sitting back and watching a movie, even though I feel myself breathing. The old man has stopped laughing but still the air is sort of wheezing out of my chest, or the chest I'm in right now.

I walk around the place again and I don't care about the pills anymore so I leave them on the floor. This all makes sense now, waking up in another place like this, not even finding the goddamned light switch. I wonder how long it will last and if I should lay down so I don't fall over or something. When I wake up, I mean. It would be just like me to do something stupid like that. But when I think of it I realize it must be that I'm already in my bed and that I'm only dreaming that I'm walking around in this strange place.

I go over to the bookshelf and look through the books quickly. It's a pretty good collection, if I may say so; not too many books, but most of them seem worth reading. Although, many of them I haven't even heard about. Still, I just know they are good books.

I go over to the desk and look at the pictures again. I pick each frame up and study each person closely and this time there's something about them that seems familiar, but I can't put my finger on exactly what it is. I go over to the window and try to look outside, but it's still too dark to see anything, so I simply walk around the small apartment, feeling all heavy and stiff, trying out this dream of mine.

I'm reminded again of how thirsty I am and I drink a glass of water in the kitchen and it tastes just like normal. I can even feel the icy cold liquid pour down my throat and into my stomach.

I have no idea when it will wear out, when the dream will start fading and I will wake up. Right now I feel more awake than I ever have, so I suppose I just have to wait and see.

I pinch my arm and this skin I'm in is so soft and loose that I get a good piece of it between my fingers. I don't pinch it very hard at first but then I really give it all I've got and I feel it sting. When I let go it takes a while for the skin to go back down like it was before, and when it finally does I see my fingers have left a red mark. But I'm still asleep just the same.

There's not a whole lot to do in here and I'm already pretty tired of this dream and this crummy apartment. I mean, it would have been different if it would have been any other dream, like a dream that took place in some exotic country, or a dream where I could fly or something, anything really, other than being an old man. I mean, who the hell dreams about being an old man anyway?

I go back to the bed and lay down on the cover with my arms behind my head. It feels better in my back when I lay like this. I can see through the window that it's starting to get lighter outside but from where I am I still can't see more than a steel blue soup. I close my eyes and try to go back to sleep. I figure if I close my eyes and try to walk back the exact way I came, sort of backtracking the thoughts in my head and doing everything in reverse, it might get me to where I started. It's only logical really.

So I pull the cover up, right back up under my chin, and I keep my eyes closed and think about all the madcap stuff that happened to me around last Christmas, before I got so run down I had to come out to this place to rest. I try to see my room with the two great windows, my bedside table with my notebook on it, without any lousy pills, and I try to see my bed with the squeaky springs that make this terrible sound every time you turn around in it. I even try to see the wheels that are under each foot of the bed, in case they need to push you anywhere.

They never have though; pushed me anywhere, I mean. I try to focus on all these things and feel what I felt last night, looking back at all that has happened lately. I just have to go backwards, a few steps, that's all, and I'll be back in no time.

I lay like this, picturing my room for what seems to be an eternity, but nothing happens. I open my eyes and see the top of the trees through the dusky light and I realize it's not working. I'm just too goddamned awake to fall asleep again.

Nobody is going to believe me when I tell them about this. They'll think I've gone completely crazy in this place, instead of the opposite. Not that anybody knows where I am, but still, if I tell them about it they'll just think I'm making it all up. And I suppose in a way they will be right. I mean, in a way I really am making it all up. It's my dream, isn't it?

This being a dream and all, it's strange how things can seem so real. Everything feels very real. The way my hand touches things, the way my breath stinks, and the way the day is getting brighter every time I look outside. I guess I will just have to wait for it to end by itself. All I know is I can't stay another second in this crummy bed and pretend to sleep, or I'll go crazy for real, and then I'll never leave this place. I mean, the place I'm *really* in.

I get up and go stand by the window and I watch the day break, but all I can see is a small garden and, past that, a thick forest begins. The sun is trying to break through the trees, but it's not a real sun like on a summer day; instead what rises behind the pines is more of a gray luminous mass. It's the kind of sun that has you squinting all day just to get through the dullness.

This is a real quirky feeling; I have to say. This is about the weirdest I have ever felt in my whole crummy 16-year life. This is the kind of strange dream where everything seems possible. For instance, when I look out across the garden I can see an old lady dressed in nothing but a nightgown. She's standing barefoot in the grass, moving her arms up and down from the ground, like she's hanging imaginary laundry out to dry. I'm not even surprised. At this point I wouldn't be surprised if a pink elephant with wings came flying out of the forest. I really wouldn't.

So maybe it really is one of those dreams where you can fly and walk through walls. I mean, I haven't tried it, but perhaps it is. I put my forehead to the window and then the tip of my nose and I sort of press my face against the glass harder and harder to see if I can push through it. Now, if I really do, I will freak out for sure, but at the same time it would be one hell of a thing. I move my hands up along the glass, next to my face, and every time I see them I can't believe my eyes. I use my old wrinkled knuckles to bang on the glass, but it is just as solid and has the same hollow sound as when I'm awake.

I'm so bored I go over to the desk to look at the photographs again. I pick the frames up one by one and study them closely and each time I look at them they seem more familiar than the last time, but I suppose that's only natural. One picture, the one of an older woman, I can almost swear I know from somewhere. Perhaps she's one of the nurses or something, and this is her room. But then, why would I dream about an old nurse and her room? There's a picture of another older woman I don't recognize even the slightest, then a younger one with some young kids all around her. Everybody looks sort of queer, with the funny clothes they wear and all, like they're not from around here, but from a far away place, like Germany or something.

Come to think of it, most of the things in this place seem kind of queer. Take the TV in the bookshelf for example. It's sort of weird looking in a way I can't describe, but just by looking at it I know there's something weird about it. It's the same with the kitchen and the tiny machines there. Half of them I don't even know what they are. On the counter there seems to be some sort of oven but it's very tiny and it kind of looks like the TV, in that same weird way, and when I turn the lights on in the bathroom and look at myself in the mirror once again, everything in there seems so – what's the word – sleek. Yeah, that's how all the things look, sleek. It makes me wonder where the hell this dream is being played out anyway. Perhaps I'm actually in Germany.

But it could just as well be onboard a spaceship, for all I know.

I think I can see parts of myself when I look in the mirror. I couldn't at first, but now that I keep staring at one detail at a time until my eyes go blurry, I think I can see parts of myself under all that old stuff.

Funny, I've never even imagined what it would feel like being old, so in a way I guess it's good that I can try it out now, and not only when it's too late. For all I know there are probably tons of things to learn just because you get old and need to know. I mean, the last thing I want to be when I'm old is like old Spencer, shuffling around in a robe showing everyone his goddamned chest. But I do understand him a bit better now, because of everything that's happened to me. And I don't just mean this dream, even if that helps a lot. For example, every time I bend down my knees hurt like hell and the pain in my back hasn't gone away at all, and when I try to draw a deep breath, something in my chest is blocking out the air.

I guess you could compare getting old to a deserted and run down house that nobody cares about anymore. A house that people would rather tear down, instead of fixing the creaky old floorboards and the leaky roof. But I guess you can really never understand that until you've experienced it. So in a way this dream isn't that bad after all.

Even so, when I get as old as Mr. Spencer, I will still never walk around in nothing but a crummy robe showing the whole goddamned world my wrinkled chest.

If I really feel what I feel, I have to say I haven't felt this good since I don't know when. The only thing that's bothering me right now, except being bored, is my stomach. I'm hungrier than a whole regiment of, well, I don't know what, but I'm pretty damn hungry. I'm usually not a very big eater, especially not for breakfast, but right now I think I could eat my way out of prison if it was made of bread and cheese. It feels like I haven't eaten in a decade.

I close my eyes and picture a plate filled with warm toast, scrambled eggs and bacon, along with a big glass of orange juice. I see it so clearly that I can almost smell it, but when I open my eyes I can't catch sight of it. I close my eyes and try again. This time I add some apple pie and I try to will it all onto a tray waiting for me on the table when I open my eyes. But when I do, the only thing I see on the table are the photos. Now wouldn't that be terrific, just closing your eyes and wishing for it to appear in front of you. There must be something I'm missing with this whole dream thing, like an instruction manual or something. I guess Ill just have to make do with the old system for now.

I go to the kitchen and open the tiny fridge but it's completely empty, save for some jars of stuff I wouldn't eat even if I was starving, and I mean that. When I close the door I see a paper pinned to the outside of the fridge with different colored boxes filled with text, like information about bridge and all sorts of things, and in one of the boxes it says: **Breakfast, ground floor, 7-10**. That works for me, as long as I get something to eat.

I open the closet without even trying to picture the clothes flying out and dressing me while I just stand here. I really wish this dream didn't include wearing someone else's clothes, but I guess there's not much I can do about it. I'm really not that picky when it comes to germs or things like that; it's just that I'm not too crazy about wearing other people's underwear. Call me a snob but that's how I feel, and just to let you know, I wouldn't even if this wasn't a dream.

I take what I need from the closet and get dressed. I pick a faint blue striped shirt that feels like it's been worn so many times it's become paper thin. At first I'm amazed that everything fits me just fine, but then, when I realize where I am, it doesn't seem that spectacular.

I pick the shoes that look least like an old man's shoes, which is harder than it sounds because they all do, and as I leave I make a half-hearted attempt of walking straight through the door without opening it.

I close the door behind me and come right out into a corridor. I'm guessing this place is some sort of mix between a hospital and a hotel because the carpets are really thick and the wallpaper has these big flowers on it that curl up along the wall from the floor to the ceiling. The only thing that makes it look more like a hospital than a hotel is the handrail that goes along the wall all the way to the elevator.

I hear soft music coming from somewhere above and it follows me into the elevator. There are only three buttons to choose from and I press the one for the ground floor and breakfast. Maybe after I eat I will look around and see what kind of place this really is.

I feel the elevator shake and I pray for it not to get stuck. Now, wouldn't that really take the cake – getting locked inside an elevator while being locked inside a dream? It seems funny when you first think of it, but I'm not kidding you. That sort of madcap stuff always seems to happen to me.

I look at my face in the mirror and without thinking about it my hand goes up and pushes a piece of white hair to the side. For a second I feel like myself, because that's my gesture; I do that with my hair. Then I realize I really am myself; I'm just temporarily on the other side.

I turn directly to the right as I come out of the elevator and somehow I know I should make a left and then another right to get to the breakfast room. I guess it's still pretty early and that's why I don't meet anyone else on my way there. Come to think of it, I haven't seen a single person in this dream, except for the lady in the garden.

But when I step inside the breakfast room, I see that I'm not alone. Way down by the end of the room, at the very end of a long table, I see an old man with a big round belly. He looks like quite a funny character really. His belly is so big that he can't sit all the way in under the table. He has to reach forward and strain his neck to reach the food, which he balances on a fork in front of his face. I watch him for a little bit and it's a vicious circle really. The more he eats, the bigger his belly gets, and the more he has to strain to get to his food; the more he strains the hungrier he gets and the more he has to eat. I have no idea what any of this means but I can't help thinking that it's just grand to put me in a dream in a place with a bunch of old people. I hate that world, by the way, grand.

But now that I'm here I might as well take advantage of the breakfast that is served in a parade of bowls on a long counter. I grab a plate and I start by filling it with scrambled eggs about halfway up. I continue with a layer of bacon, and then I take a stack of toast on the side and about a bucketful of butter. To go with it all I pour myself a tall glass of orange juice.

I feel sort of awkward about where to sit; there are so many empty chairs and it would be almost rude not to sit with the funny looking man, even though it is only a dream. So, I walk over to the table where he's sitting, I mean, just for the hell of it. Besides, it would actually feel nice to have some company when I eat.

When he sees me coming he nods his head towards me, almost like we know each other. I nod back and put my tray down, but I don't say anything. To tell you the truth, I'm not really too keen on this voice of mine, the way it sounds as if it's going to break down any second.

This is the first time for me, being this goddamned hungry in a dream and all. I attack my toast and my eggs and bacon with grim determination and as I shuffle truckloads of it into my mouth, my whole body starts to feel good. I finish the whole plate in like a minute or something, and during that time I don't even notice the world around me. Not even the old man on the other side of the table. That's how hungry I am.

When I'm done I don't feel so hot anymore. I must have devoured five or six eggs and as many pieces of toast, and I push the plate aside and notice that he is looking sort of curiously at me.

You sure are hungry today, C. he says. I don't think I've ever seen you eat more than a piece of toast or two before, at the most. What happened?

You run a marathon last night?

He lets out this laugh that comes way down from his belly, a laugh that makes it jump up and down, up and down, shaking the entire table.

I have no idea what he's talking about. Naturally, he's quite a character, but I have no idea what he's talking about. Perhaps this is a place where they do weird experiments on old people, like government experiments and stuff they can't do on normal, young people. I've read about places like this; they do exist.

I look at him and I try to see if he resembles anyone I know or anyone I've ever met, because that's usually what you dream about. You know, people that somehow pass through your life. It could be a lifelong friend but it could also be the mailman, or even a substitute mailman you only see for one day of your life. That sort of stuff kills me.

His face is pudgy and it kind of overflows to the sides and droops over his jaw and hangs downwards, and without staring I can actually see a couple of long straws of hair growing from the inside of his nose. I almost have to turn my face away, but then I remember that I'm old too, at least right now, and that's what happens to you when you get old. You don't really remember to cut long hairs from your nose and all that crap. I look at him and try to see under all that overflowing skin, but I really can't find anything about his face, or the rest of him for that matter, that rings a bell. He could be anybody in the world for all I know.

The next thing I do, even though I know I shouldn't, still feeling the way I do and all, being so awfully awake I mean, is to get up to get some coffee. But I do it anyway.

Look at the little rabbit, a young boy in an old man's cloak, he doesn't suspect a thing. In a way I do feel bad for him, for getting into this mess in the first place. It's really all my fault. I should have done something about this a long time ago. But then again, how could I have known?

To be honest, I'm not completely sure how this works. Even though I'm the one holding all the strings, I don't know what happens to them when we let them be without care for so long. Do they meet with others and create lives like yours and mine? Or are they simply placed inside a cocoon and awakened only when you again sharpen your pen? There are so many questions I don't have any answers to.

What I do know is that there are certain rules I have to follow. I didn't make them, but they are there all the same, and I have to follow them. There's no accounting for what will happen otherwise.

You see, this is how it works on the other side. The most important rule, the one you cannot break or go around, is that everyone here needs to have a past. It's really true everywhere but especially so here. If you don't have a past you don't exist. So I have to give him something to hang on to; I need to give him a life.

Right now he's confused, the poor boy. Who wouldn't be? But it will pass. This very moment he is nothing really but empty space. He is like a piece of paper upon which you have once started a story, and then locked in a box and buried deep in the ground. Now, 60 years later, you dig that same box up and continue the story from where the last sentence ended. So, you see how all this is confusing to him. Imagine going to sleep and the next day when you wake up it's half a century later. But I'm catching up by the second. As fast as the tiny arms can hit.

It really is a lot like playing a game of chess. I have to play the game from the start and move all the pieces in the right order, or I won't win. I can't just push the other queen off with my fingertip, no matter how much I want to, even though that would save me a lot of work. I have to follow the rules and play the entire game from the start. Since this is really the opposite of what I'm trying to do, excuse me for not being overly enthusiastic about the whole thing. But it is the only way to do it. By no means, it wasn't an easy decision, I just need him for one last thing. I have to build him from where I left off. I have to give him a past for the simple reason that you can't kill what doesn't exist.

5

I'm standing by the coffee pot when the funniest thing happens to me. The dream about the tapping, the one I told you about, the one I've had every night now for several weeks, I hear it again. I guess it's not so funny when you actually think about it. After all, this is a dream, but it still strikes me as funny, hearing it like that in the back of my mind as I pour myself a cup of coffee. Tap-tap-tap, tap-tap, tap-tappety-tap.

Harry, I begin before I have even sat down, because I just thought of something I have to tell him. I spill some of the coffee on the table, but not enough for me to have to get something to wipe it off with, I simply try to put my cup over it. It's not really a goodbye but I want to leave him with something, at least a few words, even though they don't mean anything.

Harry, do sparrows fly south in the winter?

Before he even has a chance to answer me I continue.

I mean, why do some birds decide to leave while others stay?

I can't really say why I'm asking him this – it's not like I've been thinking a whole lot about birds lately – but the question just sort of pops into my mind.

Harry rinses the last piece of toast down with some coffee and I watch his jaw muscles tighten and then relax. This is just me shooting the crap with my old friend. It doesn't really matter to me what we talk about. We could talk about dogs or whales or hubcaps for all I care, as long as we shoot the crap about something.

Harry looks straight through me at something far off in the distance without saying a word. Perhaps he knows I'm leaving. Some things you can just feel. Hell, I only just realized it myself when I woke up this morning. It's nothing I can put my finger on. I've been here long enough, but it's not only that. Somehow I just know I've gotta get out of this place.

Finally Harry talks to me.

I guess it's because small birds can't fly that far. But he keeps looking straight through me.

But it can't just be about size, I say.

Now I actually really want to know this, even though we're just shooting the crap.

Then all big birds would fly south, I say, and they don't. I mean, take the owl for example; it doesn't fly south.

Harry's got nothing more to eat and he moves a few crumbs around on his empty plate before he presses his thumb over the little pile and sucks it into his mouth.

Shucks, I don't know, C, he says. There could be a bunch of reasons why sparrows don't fly south in the winter, but I bet you one of them is that they are just too goddamned small.

Suddenly Harry stares straight at me and I see that he looks a lot older than I do, even though we are both in our late 70's.

I guess you're right, I say, because I don't feel like talking about sparrows anymore, or anything at all for that matter. It's one of those things that you don't know before you really know it, but those are the last words we ever say to each other.

I don't have that many friends here. There are really only two people at Sunnyside I ever talk to. There's old man Harry and Jimmy the gardener. Jimmy is from Mexico and, strictly speaking, he isn't really a resident, but he's here so much he might as well be. Jimmy works in the garden and he is nearly as old as anyone here but he still has the stance of a young man with leather like skin and arms, long and dry like the vines he is trimming. A moustache sprouts from his upper lip and every time I see him he has become more and more like the things he works on. I swear, one day, he's going to be gone and when they look for him they're gonna find him growing out of the same soil he turns twice a year, fertilizes and waters without even taking a break.

I watch myself in the mirror on the way up in the elevator. I brush my hair to the side and wonder if I shouldn't get a haircut soon. It's not really growing that much anymore, like the last 30 years or so, but it still feels good to get a haircut. At least for a couple of hours, a haircut makes you feel brand new.

Back in my room I walk straight over to the bed and lay down. As soon as my head hits the pillow I close my eyes. I'm not really sure why I go to bed because I'm not really sleepy at all. It's getting to be just past morning and it would be smarter if I wait until it at least gets dark before I take a nap, but nevertheless, it feels like something I have to do. Every now and then I like to lay on my back with my eyes closed and not move even a finger.

It sure is hard when you really try. Not moving even a single finger I mean. I keep myself very still but my eyes keep darting from side to side behind my closed eyelids and I have a hell of a time getting them to stay in one place. It's the same thing every time you try really hard to do something. There's a resistance inside that wants to do the opposite, no matter what it is you try to do.

But after a little while I do manage to keep absolutely still. I even manage to focus my eyes on the one spot behind my eyelids that is a bit darker than the rest. It's strange though, just as I've become perfectly still I can't even remember why I'm laying here. Come to think of it, I can't even remember what day it is. All I do know is that I should sleep for a bit and then I have to be on my way.

The moment I wake up I know things are different. An echo of it is still bouncing around in my head, trapped between the wall of dream and reality, but I can't yet believe it. It's been such a long time since I last dreamt.

I had it for the first time when I was 16. Then it lasted a couple of weeks before it went away, just like that, and I've never had it since. Maybe it's because of its nature that I remember it so vividly, or simply because this is the only dream I have ever had. I mean, I have nothing to compare it to, only that first dream when I was 16. It is a strange dream by any measure.

It's not about a person or a place, and it doesn't include pictures or voices of any kind. It's a dream about a sound, a simple tapping sound, like that of an old-fashioned typewriter being punched.

It was early morning, just like this, and I was in one of many schools, a place much like this too, actually. Suddenly, I opened my eyes and, just like that, I was awake. After that, for a couple of days, every time I woke up, the tapping stayed in my ears for a few moments. It was the strangest feeling in the world, really. I had never felt anything like it. I'm not sure how to describe it but it was similar to the feeling of waking up from a very deep and long sleep. But most of all, it was a feeling of not being lost anymore. Somehow, waking up that first day when I was 16, I knew exactly what I had to do.

The same as I do now. I sit up in bed and see through the window that it's a gray and dull day, but for once I don't feel dull. I feel like I have to get up because there's something important I have to do.

I notice I'm still wearing my clothes. It's strange how I can't remember going to bed last night, but I must have been awfully tired because I didn't even undress. The blue striped shirt that Mary gave me is all wrinkled and my skin feels hot and sticky, the way it gets when you fall asleep in your clothes, and there's this feeling inside me that I slept too long.

I walk across the room over to the window and I look outside. Today I don't see anyone out there, although sometimes it happens that I see old ladies in their nightgowns hanging imaginary laundry on imaginary summer days. At this place you can see just about anything if you're up at the right time.

But right now everything in the garden is still and I listen to the nothingness that surrounds this place. If I didn't know any better I'd think we were a million miles away from everything here. And actually, that's how it feels most of the time.

It's awfully quiet. The only sound I can hear is the sound of my own breath silently wheezing in and out of my chest. It reminds me of a second hand jutting across the surface of a clock. It's all an illusion though, because the only thing that really changes up here is the world around me. The trees, for example, all look as if they've been in a fight during the night, displaying a rainbow of colorful bruises. What was green not long ago is now red, yellow and purple.

With my life, it's different. For example, I don't remember anything before my 16th birthday. I can tell you what happened, but I don't have any memories of my own. It's the same with the rest of my life. I know where and how I met Mary, how we fell in love, how we got Daniel, and how we loved him together for so long, but still it feels like looking at a wall pinned with thousands of sun faded polaroid's. They are not my life; they're only snapshots of my life. Between the tapping dream 60 years ago and the dream last night, my life seems to have played out in a heavyset mist between two station stops.

How is that possible – to exist and not exist at the same time?

On the window right in front of my face I see a stain, some sort of smudge. First I try to rub it off with my thumb, but it doesn't work and I figure it's something on the outside. I pull the window up and stick my head out. As I lean forward the wall presses on my bladder and it hurts like hell, but I don't want to give in just yet. Eventually it always wins, but I like to give the bastard a run for it every now and then.

I look at the trees, the way they've changed color, and I feel sad. The fall always gives me the blues, and I suppose it's not just the trees. Some people say it's because of the light, but I just get this crummy feeling inside every time I see a leaf fall. They are dying, a million of them every minute, but nobody notices. I can just hear their silent screams of agony while they drift to the ground. I can be such a wimp sometimes.

Cold air pours over the ledge and sweeps into the room. First it surrounds my feet, then it rises like water in a sinking boat, and when it gets neck high it seeps into the opening of my shirt and down over my chest. It makes me shiver and I inhale deeply, hold my breath, and close my eyes.

Usually, each morning is only a continuation of the day before, as if I am stuck in the same frame of film that is repeated over and over again until someone gives the projector a violent slap and the wheel starts rolling again. For a second no thoughts enter my mind and I can't tell if I'm awake or if I'm dreaming. I let go of the grip and the air rushes out. Sometimes I really do wish life was more like a movie you could bang when it got stuck and fast forward when you wanted to get to the end.

I'm just about to pull my head back in when I see a sparrow on the ground below my window. It's dark red and painfully perfect, and it seems to be riding on a small wave of green grass. It looks so peaceful; this is how I imagine sparrows go to sleep at night. Its beak is slightly open and its wings are folded in neatly along the sides as if it's holding onto itself. Except this sparrow isn't sleeping.

So this is where the smudge came from. It must have happened sometime yesterday. I pull my head back in and get in the shower. I look through the shirts in the closet but they all fill me with disgust, the way they know I can never wear them all out, and I end up choosing a plain white one and I make my way down to the breakfast room.

6

*T*here was a time when we got along fine, but soon enough it all changed. He started waking me in the middle of the night with questions about this and that, questions that needed answers, he said. He was there when I woke and there when I fell asleep, but perhaps worst of all, he was in my dreams. There were decisions to make, turns to take, and things to become. All the choices one must make in life, all the crossroads, and he had only me to ask. He tried very hard to stay close to me, but like an animal with a new season's children, I pushed him away.

You give someone a piece of your finger, you reach

out a helping hand, you not only save their life, you create it. You are their God. But it's all or nothing. You try to take it, bite after bite of flesh until your bones begin to show, and then you just can't anymore. I did the only thing I could. I turned and faced the wall at night and willed myself to a blind and deaf sleep. I shut him out of my life, and I shut him out of his.

Still, for some time the questions didn't cease. It's not easy to undo certain things. His voice was constantly there, like a background ramble. Some days were worse than others, but I held on and I endured. I endured until eventually his voice was nothing more than a whisper in the back of my mind. By ignoring his existence, I shook him loose. It took the best of me, and what I lost I will never get back, but finally my head was empty. For a while I thought I had succeeded.

It's something to do with old age. You start around midway, with holding off on the burying of new things. You've learned better by then. Some years go to this. Then before you know it you are in the homestretch and what you've buried starts to stink. Either you haven't buried things deep enough or the rain has washed the dirt away. Any number of things can happen. The only sure thing about it is that it happens to us all. The remaining years are then spent digging up what you once buried and making things done wrong, right. It's an endless trip back and forth to the cemetery, until one day you finally go there and don't come back.

I'm running out of time here and I need to be able to breathe air that doesn't stink, just for a little while. I need these few gasps of freedom before I go. I should have done this a long time ago. I should have done with him just what Shelley did to her monster, so now, I will wipe my slates clean and finish what I've started. And that's the irony of it all. I worked so hard to get him to leave me alone, and now I'm the one bringing him back just so that I can kill him.

Old man Harry is always the first one down for breakfast because he likes eating more than he likes sleeping. When I come down he's sitting in a chair all by himself. I'm not really that hungry but I take a piece of toast and a glass of orange juice from the long table and sit down opposite him. Harry is very still and the only thing that really moves is the high stacked tower of wobbling orange jelly piled on a piece of toast paused in front of his face.

We never say much and I listen to the clock on the wall and the sound Harry's nose makes every time he chews. I'm already gone. It's not going to be hard to leave this place. I do feel sorry for Harry though. I mean, from now on he will be eating alone.

Harry, I begin.

It's not a goodbye but I want to leave him with something, at least a few words.

Do sparrows fly south in the winter?

I don't know why I want to know about the sparrows, there's no particular reason, the words just come out that way.

Harry coughs and a small piece of jelly toast flies out and lands on the table between us.

For christsakes, haven't you dropped the sparrows yet! For christsakes!

I have no idea what's gotten into him. I guess he's just having one of those mornings when he's impossible to talk to.

I was just saying, I say, I wonder why some birds decide to leave and some don't.

But I say the last part very low because I don't want to upset Harry anymore before I leave him. I see how agitated he looks already. His face is flushed pink and he still coughs every now and then as if there's a piece of something tickling his throat.

I'm not really hungry. I've never been a big eater after all, and I push my plate to the side. Suddenly I feel I have to get the hell out of there right away. Not because of Harry or anything but just because that's how I feel.

Back in my room I sit down on the bed for a little bit. I look around and see the things I have seen so many times before. The desk, the picture frames with Mary, Daniel and his family, Phoebe and her kids, and I see the hats on top of my closet and the pills on my bedside table.

There should be three bottles of pills on my bedside table, each one for something Dr. Rosen wants to fix about me, but now I only see two. I must have put the other one in the bathroom. The one with the yellow lid is for my bladder, the one with the blue lid is for the dizziness, and the one with the white lid is for depression.

He is a young man, Dr. Rosen, with sad eyes that remind me of a labrador we once had. I'm not sure exactly when we had him, but I know we did. His name was Rudolph and he was with us for 4 years before he got hit by a car.

He hasn't been at it too long, Dr. Rosen, that is. He and his wife decided to move up here so they could raise their daughters in the countryside. They are all lined up on his desk, in picture frames facing him. I think doctors learn this in medical school, to keep their family in a framed row on their desk. That way, when patients see them, they think nothing bad can happen to them. Not with the doctor's family watching and all. Anyway, he has come to the right place. If there is one thing we have plenty of up here it's countryside.

I pick up the bottle with the yellow lid, but I don't open it. I just twirl it around slowly so the pills inside tumble and create an eerie sound. I can see the smudge on the window from where I'm sitting and I imagine what it would be like waking up from a night's sleep, flying out from the thick of the forest, across a garden, and smack! into an invisible wall. Gone before I even hit the ground. It sure would be a crummy way to go.

I feel sort of restless and can't sit still, so I get up, open the window again, and look down at the sparrow. I notice the world isn't completely silent anymore. I hear the wind move through the top of the trees and the house making a distant hissing noise. Suddenly I feel sad for Dr. Rosen. It comes at me from somewhere below, just like a bubble floating up, and the reason I feel sad is because Dr. Rosen will be upset when he finds out that I left without his pills.

But I don't need the pills anymore; I feel too good. Besides, I'm not planning on bringing a bag and I'd rather not carry around three bottles of pills in my pockets.

Since I'm not packing I don't have anything special I have to do, I simply take the navy blue jacket from the closet and hang a scarf around my neck and the last thing I do, as I pass it on my way out, is to look myself in the mirror.

I almost stumble backwards. It's not because of how I look or anything. My clothes are fine and my white hair is combed to the side. What startles me is the look in my eyes. They have that same half-crazy look a captain standing in the bow of his ship has when looking at an oncoming storm. Part of him is saying,

Oh shit, and another part, Come and get me.

But it's mostly the smile that does it. The crusty, half-crooked smile bending half my mouth out of shape. Perhaps it's because I haven't seen one there in such a long time that makes it look misplaced on my face. But I just can't help but smile as I turn and leave.

7

W hen you first see it, coming up the driveway, I guess it looks alright. It's a cream colored house crowned with a slanted Victorian roof that makes it look just like a creamy cake. There's a garden going around the back and towards the forest in the east there's a tennis court. I have never seen anyone use it though, except for when the weather is nice and they pull out the deckchairs and place them all over the court. I guess they figured we'd be younger old people.

Then there's the glassed in dining room, the library, the shuffleboard court, the pottery room, the piano bar, the indoor waterfall, the stargazing room, the reception area, and of course, the driveway. It's actually the smoothest paved road you can imagine. Not something you'd expect to find in the middle of nowhere. I'm sure it was once just a gravel road, I figure the only reason they paved it in the first place was so that when your children dropped you off they would say,

See how well they take care of this road? Imagine how well they are going to take care of you!

Just to give you an idea of what kind of place this is, I'll tell you about the path. In the garden in the back they have paved a path around the bushes and built a shelter at the end that looks just like a bus stop. Patients walk the path to get to the shelter and when they get there they sit down on their strollers and wait for the bus. They talk to each other, some to themselves, and they wait for hours, day after day, never remembering from one day to the next that there *is* no bus. Around lunchtime staff members will walk the same path and bring back those who haven't already tired of waiting. Then, after lunch, you can see them out on the path again, hurrying in slow motion around the bends to get to the bus stop in time. I suppose it isn't meant as a joke, but to me it has always seemed cruel, the way they keep chasing after that bus that doesn't exist. Anyway, that's just the kind of place this is.

Sunnyside isn't supposed to be just any old retirement home. Most of the people here are very particular about what impression they make. I mean, a lot of them piss their pants but they are still very particular about things. If you want to be cynical about it, the truth is we are here for practical reasons. Although, at Sunnyside there are hardly any practicalities when it comes down to it.

Take the day they came for Mr. Alexander; it hardly even slowed down. Sure, at dinnertime it was more quiet than usual, until one of the ladies up front started talking, and soon another lady started in, and another, and in no time everything was back to normal again. A couple of hours later it was as if Mr. Alexander had never even existed. The unspoken rule at Sunnyside is that you never talk about those who don't come down for dinner.

When I first arrived I already knew what it was called, but the sign outside the entrance still caught me by surprise. It is one of those wooden things, with dark letters burnt in by hand, probably by one of the residents in the woodshop. The sign reads: **Sunnyside – a home better than home.** I have never heard such a phony thing in my life. First of all, nobody *wants* to go to Sunnyside. You are *sent* here. And it sure as hell doesn't feel like home. Besides, you only come here for one thing and I think of all the places in the world, Sunnyside is the worst place to die.

But you see, that's just the thing about

Sunnyside. It's a place built to be something young people expect old people to like. All in all, Sunnyside isn't just another phony place, it's a place like all the others. There are no places left to go. This is it. And that's what really kills me.

We first spoke about it the day after Christmas. I was in his house in California. The two of us hadn't been alone together since I can't even remember and then suddenly we sat across from each other in his study. He was behind his desk and I was in a chair facing him. I saw there was something under his hand and he saw me noticing it.

This is the best place, Dad, he said, and I didn't see the point in arguing.

When the pressure gets too high, all air wheezes out of me. All my life I have been a flat tire.

Ahhhhh! I can already feel it, how the stench is beginning to clear. I can finally breathe again. I'm catching up with him and he is now well on his way. There's not much to it actually; you just have to give it a push in the very beginning and then the ball starts rolling all by its pretty self. I simply put my fingers on the keys and they dance joyfully without my interference. It's really as if they still remember.

Now, I will just wait for the right moment and then it will all be over.

Someone once said, "The hardest part doesn't lay in the doing, but in the thinking," and I'm bound to agree. It makes me wonder if a story is ever really created or the story itself is the creator, but I guess now is no time for such a voyage of introspection.

The same old elevator music is playing in the corridor. Usually it drives me nuts, but now somehow it doesn't bother me anymore. I don't look back or anything. I just pat my chest to make sure that the lump that is my wallet is there, and that's it. I can't think of anything else I will need.

The thought of leaving is now so strong that I don't bother to wait for the elevator. I use the stairs and come out directly into the lobby. The girl behind the counter, Anna, she's the only one of them I like. I guess the reason is because she is always very polite and her smile is the most natural thing in the world. I suppose it doesn't hurt that she's also very pretty. She looks up when I step through the door, and she smiles at me this time too.

It's a nice day for a walk, Mr. C, she says, and she does it in a way that makes you feel that she really means it.

Things like that used to kill me, but they don't so much anymore.

I haven't planned on stopping and I don't know why I do. I really want to leave right away.

But there is this word on my tongue that wants out but can't decide if it should go or not. I stand there on the other side of the desk for a couple of seconds, slowly swaying back and forth. I can hardly even feel the floor under my feet. Anna and I look at each other and I think she is about to say something, perhaps repeat herself, but she only looks at me and smiles her sweet smile.

Cunt. The word just pops into my head. I'm surprised. Even though I've always been a big swearer I can't see why I would think of a word like that at this moment. *Cunt.* I notice that Anna is looking at me differently now; her face is all flushed and her eyes are dark and bullet like. My whole insides are itching and it's really getting warm under my wool jacket, so I start walking towards the entrance.

The last words I utter as I walk through the front door just come to me.

I'm flying south. If you could tell Harry.

It really is a gray day. The sky is covered in a monster of a cloud and it hangs threateningly low, suffocating the sound of my shoes against the road before it has a chance to go anywhere. It only takes me five minutes to walk down to the gravel road that cuts like a wire through the forest out to the main road, but it feels like forever.

I really have no idea when the bus is coming; I've never had a reason to take it before. I just know there is one.

I stand by the side of the road and wait. I feel the chill from the wind and button my jacket and already I can think of something I forgot to bring. My gloves. My hands are ice cold and I shove them deep inside my pockets and I lean out and look in both directions for the bus, but I'm not even sure which way it's coming from.

Now that I'm leaving this place I begin to notice all sorts of things I haven't noticed before, like the old mailbox just inside the entrance. They can't have put it up just recently; it looks way too old for that, but I am sure I've never seen it before. I sort of feel sorry for it. Its red paint has dried and some of it is falling off in large flakes, revealing the rusty metal underneath. It has all sorts of dents and bruises and has sunken down in the middle, as if it no longer has the strength to stay upright. It must have been put up a long time ago, back when this place was still a farm. I know I shouldn't, feel sorry for it I mean, but it looks so damn lonely where it stands.

I walk up to it, mostly because it feels better to move than it does to stand still, and even though the numbers have faded I can still make them out.

Nineteen fifty-one.

Right then I hear a sound in the distance, the sound of an old diesel engine chugging through the forest. I step into the road but not until he is close enough to see me standing there waving my freezing hands does the driver let go of the accelerator.

I take a seat in the middle of the bus and as we pull away I keep my eyes glued to the old mailbox as long as I can. Nineteen fifty-one. I don't know if it means a goddamn thing, but it just so happens to be the year I left another place.

It doesn't take long before it starts to rain. The bus stops to pick up passengers along the way and every time it does I watch the drops of water move sideways across the window as the bus accelerates. More and more people get on until it's almost full. Soon the air is dense with the smell of wet clothes, and the floor is filled with dripping umbrellas. We pull up onto the freeway and the rain keeps falling, but now none of the drops make it as far as the window. They are smashed into a mist by the turbulence. I close my eyes and try to think about the last time I left for New York.

It was a chilly day. I remember because someone had swiped my brand new leather gloves directly from my coat pocket, and I was freezing my goddamned fingers off. Stuff like that could drive my parents crazy, me losing my stuff everywhere, but it's not like it was my fault.

I was standing on a hill watching the soccer game being played below. Next to me stood an old cannon, massive and black as tar, and the players looked tiny from where I was standing. I was really on my way to say goodbye to an old aquaintance, but I stopped on the way to smoke a cigarette and watch the players for a minute. It's not like I was in a rush or anything, I wasn't planning on ever coming back. So, I kept watching the game and smoked a couple of cigarettes until my head felt dizzy and I got the feeling that it would be enough for me to take just one giant step and crush them all under my foot.

8

I made him once; I cast him in my own blood. In a way he is my son, my property, at any rate. Yet, I won't mourn him when he's gone. For such a long time he's been a burden to me, he's been a boulder anchored to my leg. Wherever I've gone I've had to struggle, and when I finally got where I was going, he'd be right there with me. It's a hell of a thing and, no, I won't mourn him.

I intend to be fast and swift. My time is running out and this time I will leave nothing to chance. I've taken him back to the place I know best, to the same streets where I once brought him to life. Here the possibilities are endless.

I see him sitting in a café not far from the bus station, waiting for me to whistle my tune. But I must be careful and watch my every step. I mustn't fall in the trap to keep him going around just another corner and another to see what we find. This time it's not a game, like the first time. I will have to be fast and swift. Before the ink has dried, I cannot relax.

Once upon a time I sold my soul to the devil for a golden goose. I've been paying for it ever since. It's taken me years to figure a way to get out. He doesn't give back what you've once given him and there's no way to strike a deal with that bearded goat. The only thing you can really do is catch him by surprise. You need to fuck the devil when he least expects it, and I think I've found a way. I think I've found a way to fuck the devil, and I will now do what I ought to have done a long time ago.

I'm sitting in a café not far from the bus station. The bus arrived a couple of hours ago so now I'm in this café, watching the rain ride high on the waves of wind and roll through the streets of New York. I guess I should have some sort of plan, but I really don't know where to start.

I suppose I should write to my son about it – let him know I've left – but the problem is, and I'm ashamed to say it, we have never really been that close. I don't know if the reason is that I've always had this queer feeling of being detached from the world, from all that's in it, or if we are simply just two different people, him and I.

I never did manage to show him the way in life very well. Of course, that's one of the things I would change if I could go back and do it all over again. But somehow he did it just fine on his own.

It's strange how he's really the most grown up of the two of us. Still, I can't picture him receiving such a letter from his father.

Dear son, I've gone away on a whim. I wasn't kicked out; I went because I felt I had to. I don't know what I will do, but it doesn't matter. Whatever happens will be fine. Dad.

And that's true. It really doesn't matter.

All I'm saying is, I suppose I should write my son about it, but I know I won't.

A wet leaf is stuck to the outside of the window. I sit and watch it and the occasional wanderer hurry by in the rain as I sip my coffee. You can make a cup of coffee last a long time this way. Really, anything that you just do while not doing anything else, and I mean nothing else, you can make last a long time. If you don't know what I mean you should try it sometime.

I don't suspect anybody knows yet where I am. I don't even think they've started missing me. Perhaps tomorrow, or even tonight, but not right now. Right now it's like I don't exist.

I feel sort of naked because in the coat on the chair next to me I have everything I brought with me. Not that I had that much to begin with, but now this is all I have. I'm starting to think that I should at least have packed a small bag, a pair of underwear and a toothbrush, things like that, but I guess I'll be fine.

I haven't decided exactly what I will do here. Perhaps I'll look up some old friends and take it from there. I figure if I sit here long enough it will come to me. Meanwhile, I watch the leaf on the window and slowly sip my coffee.

Eventually the rain eases off and I step outside. I pick one direction and start walking because it doesn't really matter which way I go. What matters is that I'm back in New York and that, once again, everything is possible. I think if I just go with the flow it will find me when it's ready. And perhaps that's the point right there – the simple act of not knowing what to do next. Like right now, I'm just an empty bag blowing in the wind, and I'm starting to feel good about this whole thing.

I know I'm walking west but I force myself not to look at the street signs, so I can't say exactly where I am. I look at everything I pass with great interest and I can't recall ever being in this neighborhood before, even though I'm sure I have. I pass little shops that sell little things and I remember back when it used to be that bigger was better. These days it's all about time, about making a minute here and there. Time has made everything smaller, except buildings, and in ten years, who knows if you can even step into a phone booth and pick up a normal telephone.

I come to a crossing and stop to wait for the light to turn green. When it does, I let the couple in front of me take the lead. I just look straight ahead and don't even bother looking around as I step into the street. That's why I don't see it coming. I never even hear it.

The truck is huge. It's the kind you see parked outside construction sites and it comes straight out of nowhere, silent as a deadly serpent. The only thing I notice is the vibrations in the ground and the second I look up all I see is a blur of green as it passes within an inch of my shoulder. I'm almost sucked into the turbulence that follows behind it but somehow I manage to stay upright. I spin around like a goddamned revolving sign and watch the truck disappear down the street, still without making a sound.

The signal is about to change again, and I turn quickly and look up the street before I hurry across. My hand is shaking and I hold onto the lamppost to steady myself. I feel my old heart beating hard and heavy in my chest and I look around for a place to sit down for a minute to catch my breath. There's an opening in the gate a few steps up the sidewalk and I step inside. It's some sort of community garden and I take a seat on a bench under a bougainvillea that was once probably majestic, but now looks mostly gray. That was really a close call, about as close as you ever want it. Any closer and I would have been Chop suey.

Like always, it comes afterwards. I feel like screaming at the stupid bastard that almost killed me. He probably never even saw me, and I bet he wouldn't even have noticed if he *had* run me over. His buddies at the construction site would have had to pry me out of the grill and hold me up for him to have noticed.

I take a deep breath and let it trickle out slowly. That's the only way to get rid of stress and anger; you really just have to breathe it out and let your insides become calm again. I can see the headlines clearly in front of me.

Old man makes a go for it and leaves retirement home without notice, killed by ten-ton truck the very same day. Man believed to have been confused.

Imagine the irony. Then what would have been the point of anything? And the sad part is that it wouldn't even have been the headlines, only a few words somewhere off to the side before the sports section.

That last bit I add because it's true. It's in my genes. Starting with my sister Phoebe, confusion really does run in the family.

I'm sitting in a café not far from the bus station. The bus arrived a couple of hours ago and now I'm in this café, watching the rain ride high on the waves of wind and roll through the streets of New York. I'm trying to think of what to do next, or where to go, but I'm confident that time will show me eventually. Right now, to be honest, I haven't got a clue. Even so, it feels good to be back in the city. The city has always had something to show me.

The rain has finally stopped and I walk east towards Times Square. As I walk I start thinking of my sister Phoebe. We haven't seen each other in a long time and coming to New York makes me realize how much I actually miss her. We lost contact after Mary died; I suppose it was mostly my fault. Not that it's easy to keep contact with Phoebe – the way she is most of the time and all – but I'm still her big brother. I should really have tried harder. It worked alright when Mary was around, but then again, most things were easier when Mary was still here.

I doubt that she misses me as much as I miss her though. Most of the time Phoebe doesn't even have a past to miss. On a good day she will remember your name and who you are, but on a bad day you might as well be a lamppost. Even though I've been pretty lousy at keeping in touch with her I've always kept her with me all this time, inside my head and inside my heart. When you think of it, it's really as if we have the same disorder, the two of us. Neither of us remembers the other one, even though we are in there somewhere.

She saved me once, you know. I really was going to leave. But she knew a way to my heart. I guess for her it's not so bad, having only a few blank spots where there used to be memory. I mean, how can you miss what you can't even remember? She used to live with her daughter but one day she began walking out of the house in the middle of the night. They found her on the interstate expressway in her nightgown; she was on her way to the grocery store. I guess that's when she became more than a handful.

She used to kill me, she really did. She was the cutest girl on the playground. Not only that, she was smart too. Just the way she saved me shows you how smart she really was. Any time at night I could walk into her room, if I felt like talking, and she would never get cross with me, never even once. She would only rub her eyes and sit up straight with her back against the bedpost, straight as a nail, and watch me pace back and forth across the room. I'm telling you, she was one helluva sweet kid.

Times Square is crowded as usual and I hurry across, leaving it behind me as fast as I can. I keep walking and glance into shop windows at nothing in particular and I think about nothing in particular. I am just happy to feel the rush of things around me again. I get all the way over to Park Avenue before

I have to stop to wait for a green light.

It only takes one look for me to see that the man standing on the cement divider between the different lanes is crazy. Even if his hair wasn't so long and tangled and his clothes so worn and dirty, something about his aura and the way he's holding himself up gives him away. When it turns green I start walking, and as I step onto the island I notice that his lips are moving at an incredible speed. I hear some sort of mumble and figure he is talking to himself, but it goes so fast I can't make out one single word he's saying. His rambling has become one long humming tone instead of real sentences.

I walk past him and continue to begin crossing the next section. As I step onto the crosswalk I hear the man let out a loud shriek behind me, it's like a high pitched laughter that dies down just as quickly and immediately goes back to the humming. I turn to see what he's up to and that's the reason I'm one second slower stepping out into the street, and that's why the truck misses me by an inch. I don't really get a clear view of either the truck or the man; my eyes only make it sort of halfway between them both, and all I see is the MetLife building big and heavy to my right. The truck is just a blur to one side and I can feel the wind on my face as it passes. It's one of those ten-ton trucks you see at construction sites and I'm amazed I didn't hear it coming. The bastard ran a red light and nearly killed me, but those trucks you can usually hear coming from a mile away.

I'm all shook up and my feet somehow need to keep moving and I keep walking across to the other side. There I have to take a moment because my hands are really shaking and my heart is racing like crazy inside my chest. I lean against the traffic light to catch my breath. I turn my head and I can see that the man is still standing there. His lips have stopped moving and now he's pointing a finger at me and smiling. He's moving his body rhythmically, as if he had on headphones filled with some jazzy music, and his finger sways in the air along with him. I can't help but smile and point my own finger right back at him. That crazy bastard actually saved my life.

I'm sitting in a café not far from the bus station. The bus arrived a couple of hours ago and now I'm in this café, watching the rain ride high on the waves of wind and roll through the streets of New York. I feel pretty good about being here, not especially in this café, but back in the city. This is really where I belong. I can feel it now that I'm here, how much I've missed this place, even though I don't know exactly what my next move will be. But I'm not worried. I'm sure I will think of something.

I finish my second cup of coffee just as the rain eases off and by the time I get my coat on and step through the door it has stopped completely. I start heading south for no particular reason; more than that I just feel like walking. It's been a while since I walked the streets of New York and I want to get out there and smell the fumes and hear the taxis honking once again.

As I stand on the corner outside Macy's, waiting for the light to turn, I see it coming from a distance. It's a big old truck with a flat bed, the kind they use at construction sites to carry away junk, and it hammers straight at me. The driver must have fallen asleep or something because I'm standing way up on the sidewalk, and it's one of those temporary bubbles in traffic, you know, where there are almost no other cars around even though it's in the middle of the day, and like a bat out of hell this madman truck comes shooting right towards where I'm standing. I'm lucky that I keep my eyes open and catch it coming from a distance. Without thinking I take a quick step back and push up against the wall and, just in time, I manage to get out of the way. The truck misses me by a hair or so but it clips the garbage can on the sidewalk and hurls it high into the air with a funny sounding pop. I see it in slow motion, flying in an arc through the air, landing on its side in almost the exact same spot it was standing before, although now it no longer looks like a garbage can. It looks more like an empty soda can a sports jock has smashed against his own head at some fraternity party.

If that had been my head instead, smashed against the truck, I would have been dead three times over. I feel my heart only now catching up to reality, beating hard inside my chest, and when I lift my hand and hold it in front of my face, my fingers tingle.

I've read about this sort of thing happening before, and it really does occur more often than you would think. Sometimes, to save a buck or two, they hire immigrants without papers or even a valid driver's license, and then they make them work long hours for lousy pay. But I've never seen it with my own eyes before, or been this close to being mauled myself for that matter.

The truck didn't even stop and has disappeared into the distance. Once again the streets fill with cars, as if they were all just waiting around the corner for their cue to come on out. I stand where I am, with the wall against my back because it feels safe, and I watch the light change five times before I straighten up and finally walk across. I had almost forgotten about the goddamned crazy drivers in this city. Somebody really ought to do something about them.

9

I'm sitting in a café not far from the bus station. The bus arrived a couple of hours ago and now I'm in this café, watching the rain ride high on the waves of wind and roll through the streets of New York. I feel like I should keep moving; even though I'm now where I belong, I still feel like I should keep going somewhere.

I don't bother to wait for the rain to stop; I don't even finish my cup of coffee. Instead I pull my collar up and step outside. I walk north towards the park, because that's about the only place I can think of, and by the time I get there it has stopped raining.

Something has changed about the park and it only takes me a few minutes to realize that the last time I was here the trees seemed bigger. I wouldn't swear to it, if my life depended on it I mean, but it's damn close. I walk though the park and the trees loom above me like hunched over midgets and if I tried I bet I could reach up and touch them with my hand.

Drops fall from the branches all around me and here in the park is sounds as if it's still raining. I keep walking and go up past the Met and then the Guggenheim, until eventually I come to the place below the reservoir where joggers gather in small groups. I can't shake this feeling that there's somewhere I should be heading, so I stop for a while to see if I can figure it out. Besides, I don't feel like walking around the reservoir right now.

If you catch me at the right time and day, when I'm really up for it, walking is all I really want to do. Other times I'd rather not move an inch. Let me tell you, I've done a helluva lot of walking in my life. Sometimes it seems that walking has been the only thing I've really been good at. I know it sounds phony as hell, but sometimes I really wish it would have been something else. You know, something useful. But I guess certain things are not for choosing. Anyway, right this very moment I don't feel like taking another step, so I just stand by the railing and watch the water for a little while.

I watch the afternoon sun work its way down and by the time it's taken on a brighter orange, almost red color, I start walking again. I exit the park at 86th Street and cross over to the other side. I continue to walk, first towards the east and then south. I really just walk without any place in mind and it's mostly my legs that do the walking. What I mean is, my mind is only following along, not thinking about anything in particular. The only thing I'm sort of keeping my eyes out for is a hotel where I can stay for the night. Perhaps that's why, because I'm looking for something, when I look up I find myself only one block from our old place.

I know it's not on purpose and I have no idea how I managed to walk over here without even realizing it, but as I look up I'm standing right in front of a block that represents a huge chunk of my life. Images of cars, stop signs, bricks and crosswalks are embedded somewhere in my memory, and deep inside my spine I feel them wiggle. I keep walking, and the closer I get the more they wiggle loose and come back to me, one by one. Everyday for many years I walked these streets; I grew older with them, just like the trees lining the sidewalk. I don't think I'm making it up, but then again, I can't see how it's possible to remember something like that. I look at the cracks in the sidewalk, and it could be that they are just ordinary cracks, but as I step over them I can almost swear they make sense to me. For a second I stop and close my eyes and I picture our old building, how the air conditioning units on the facade sat in a way that created a certain pattern. I'm not sure why I would even remember something like that when other things are so faded and dim.

I keep walking, now very slowly because it's just this one block. I really want it to last as long as possible and I take in all the details with great care. I'm taking a stroll through history. I see lights on in windows all around me and I imagine families gathered around dinner tables, telling stories from the schoolyard or an eventful commute, just like we once did. When I reach our building I'm not sure what to do. I know I should just walk by and leave it behind me. After all, I have nothing to do here. Still, I stop at the curb outside the door.

I don't have to count the stories, but I do anyway. One, two, three, four, five, six, seven, eight, nine, ten, eleven, twelve and fourteen. I look at our window and wonder how many times before I have been standing exactly where I'm standing now, waving goodbyes and smiling hellos. I think most of them have been happy.

I move a bit closer to the door, just so I can once again get the feeling of coming home, and I sit for a minute on the ledge going around the flowerbed. There's a small sign stuck in the soil.

No dogs in flowerbed, it says. The sign must be new because I can't remember it ever being there before, and it makes me wonder what else has changed. For example, I wonder if Joe still works the door. I turn to get a better look inside but the lobby is empty and at the moment I can't see anyone at all in there. I really wouldn't mind seeing Joe again, after all these years. Everyday for ten years you see someone and then one day it all changes. Nobody ever tells you this, but moving is the same as dying a little, and that's a fact. Every time I've moved I've left something behind, or someone. And you can't always say exactly what you've lost until later.

I get up – no, I feel myself get up is more like it – and I walk up to the front door. The doors glide open and I don't have time to think about a reason because it's still that same swooshing sound, a swooshing that takes me back in time, and I step inside.

I couldn't see him from where I was sitting, but a doorman is standing behind the counter. It's not Joe though, and I just nod towards him without stopping, walking directly over to the elevator. As I press the button I act as if I know where I'm going. When you do something you shouldn't that usually works, pretending like you own the place, walking with your head held high and all that crap. It does this time too. He gives me a nod back and then continues to read his paper, and I step into the elevator.

The lights on the strip above my head are the same as I remember them. They climb from left to right, one step at a time, thirteen heartbeats in total. One for each floor. The elevator stops but my heart keeps beating, and again, without thinking, my body gets out and I walk up to our old door. I'm curious when I see my finger reaching out, to find out where it's going, and then suddenly I'm more scared than anything when it presses the button. Everything around me is sort of distant and not really part of this moment. I look at our old door that way you look at things when you come to a new place, when all the details stand out in your mind. I realize I have never really looked at our door before, not in this way. I mean, there never was any reason for me to stand outside and look at it like some stranger. I try to hear any sounds coming from inside but the only thing I hear is my own lousy breath, and I'm just about to turn around and leave when the door opens and a woman's face appears in the gap.

She's about middle aged and has fiercely red hair, but the very first thing I notice about her isn't her hair, but her freckles. They cover her skin completely. They are all over her lips, her cheeks, her forehead, even her ears, and they match the color of her curly hair perfectly, in a way that you'd think they were all somehow part of each other. I see that her mouth is moving but she can't be speaking because I can't hear her making any sounds. At first I think something is wrong with my ears and I swallow hard to pop them, but then I realize she's not speaking at all, only chewing on something.

Her glasses move up and down to the rhythm of her jaws and I see tiny muscles relax and contract all the way up to the sides of her forehead.

I haven't prepared anything to say and frankly, I'm a bit caught off guard, so I just stand there like a fool without saying a word.

Yes?

Finally she's done chewing. She peers at me over the rim of her glasses and there's a stern softness in the way she's looking me over. She's not a bad person; that's about all I can tell.

I swallow and imagine what my old face must look like, looking back at her.

I'm looking for someone, I say, but as soon as I do I change my mind.

I mean, we used to live here.

Her eyes don't leave me and she keeps looking me up and down, probably trying to decide whether or not to call the doorman.

This used to be our place, I say.

I see her face disappear from the gap as fast as it appeared and then the door slams shut. I stand there, all of the sudden feeling very lonely, left with nothing but my last sentence hanging, cut off in the air, when, just as suddenly, I hear the chain being pulled to the side, and the next thing I know I'm standing in our old hallway.

It's all so overwhelming and I can only begin to tell her before I feel a dreary tiredness come over me. I can't piece together exactly what it is I want to say, mostly because I don't know why I'm even here, but also because I can hardly even stand on my feet anymore. I feel her firm grip under my arm as I take step after step, careful not to go too fast, and as soon as I lay down I pass out cold.

When I wake up I'm in Daniel's room. I'm on a bed and I recognize the ceiling, even though everything else is different. The echo from the tapping dream still lingers in my mind but I'm not surprised this time. I mean, I am surprised, but at the same time it feels good inside, like there's finally an order there, and I close my eyes and try to hear it again.

It's a summer day and Daniel pretends he is a rocket ship. He runs around the entire apartment, starting from the kitchen. He races through the living room, the hallway and our bedroom and ends his voyage by slipping on the edge of the carpet and hitting his chin on the toilet bowl in the bathroom. I sleep next to him several nights after that and every time I wake up the first thing I see is this ceiling. I open my eyes again. Even now it still smells like him, the way he smelled when he was a little boy.

I sit up and swing my legs out and place my feet on the floor. I rest my head in my palms for a little bit, just enough so it won't spin so damn much when I stand up. My mouth is very dry. I get up and walk to the kitchen and look for the glasses in the first cupboard, where we used to keep them, but I only find dinner plates there. I have to open all the cupboard doors before I find what I'm looking for in the very last one. My bladder is screaming at me from inside and I make my way to the bathroom. When I get out she's standing there, once again peering at me over the rim of her glasses.

I'm sorry, I say.

I'm not sure for what, but it feels like the right thing to say.

While she's making coffee I walk around the apartment and I notice how things have changed. Not that I hadn't expected them to, but it still comes as a surprise to see it this way. The only thing that has remained the same is the floor. The old wooden floor with worn patches, smooth as skin, is exactly as I remember it. It was actually the very reason we chose this apartment in the first place. Gliding over it made you feel like being a captain on your own ship.

The woman lets me walk around pretty much by myself, but I feel her watching me from behind. She seems more nervous today than last night, but I'm grateful that she gives me room to sift through the past like this.

I stop in the living room and look down at the sidewalk. I touch the wood going along the edge of the window with my fingers. Mary must have leaned on this a thousand times when she waved to me. Every weekday morning for years. I guess it's not amazing that it still feels warm.

How dare he! I have no finger in this little game of his. I have no part in this unauthorized visit to the past, this stroll along memory lane. Boo-hoo, fucking breaks my heart. He's walking through a past that isn't real, looking back at a life that has not even been lived. He's trapped in an illusion that his life is as real as anyone else's!

What an arrogant little shit! Who does he think he is? My creation, a piece of living art, seems to have grown a will of its own. I can't see how, but it's completely out of bounds. There must be a detail somewhere I've overlooked. I won't stand for it.

I go back to my room, to Daniel's room, or I guess it's really the freckled woman's room, and I sit on the bed. I look around and I have this strange feeling again that I'm supposed to be looking for something. I'm not sure exactly what, but I just know this something wants me on my feet.

I take one last look around, knowing I will never come back here again. I straighten out the sheets, pull the cover up and make the bed as perfectly as I can before I leave. When I get to the door, she's already standing there.

Before she has a chance to say anything I ask her.

Do you know if Joe is still around?

I'm hoping she will tell me he is doing fine, that he's just out in the back delivering some packages, but the look on her face tells me she has no idea who I'm talking about.

It was a long time ago, I mumble and reach for my things.

As I wait for the elevator, forever shut out from a life that used to be, I can't help but think of Joe, buried ten feet under, wrapped in his big doorman coat.

I walk from the house as quickly as I can and only when I'm two whole blocks away can I relax again. There's something really depressing about looking back at the past like that. I don't know why, but I guess it's because somehow it never really matches the memories you have in your head. It's always a few frames off.

I keep walking and I think it's somewhere around the 60's where I turn left and cross the street. An old lady is standing on the other side and as I reach the sidewalk I nod and say a good day to her, but I don't think she hears me because she doesn't nod back. That's the thing about old people; most of them just don't care anymore. I've thought about it before but it's really only when I pass the old lady that it becomes clear to me. After a certain age you just stop caring. It's a terrible thing really, but it's true. Old people like that – I bet you could set them on fire and they wouldn't even scream.

I keep walking straight ahead when suddenly a loud crash behind me makes me jump ten feet straight up in the air. It's really one hell of a crash and when I spin around I see a big piece of metal from the scaffolding above laying on the sidewalk behind me. It's only a couple of inches from where I'm standing. It has come down with such force that it has made a dent in the cement and tiny cracks spread out all over it in a spider web pattern. I look back and see the old lady standing there, still looking across the street as if it was quite normal that metal fell from the sky. It could be that she's just deaf, but I bet you she's one of those old people who wouldn't care one way or the other if she went up in flames.

I bend backwards and look up to try and see if the whole construction is about to come down. I even tug on the ground poles but they seem sturdy enough and nothing else moves except a piece of the plastic cover that flaps in the wind twenty feet up. I look back down at the cracked sidewalk and I don't know if I should laugh or cry. I really don't.

10

Half of the time I don't know why I do the things I do. I mean, after seeing that place and then almost getting smashed into smithereens by that piece of metal, I really feel like talking to someone. Someone I know. I walk on and when I turn the corner the first thing I see is a couple of phone booths. First I pass them, but then, like I said, without actually deciding to, I stop and go back.

The first booth doesn't have one but in the next one I find what I'm looking for. I pull it out and put it on the counter and open it up under C.

He's not in there, I know he's not. It's not even the same state, but I want to go through the motions just the same.

I need to let him know I'm ok. I should tell him how much I love him. Or at least I should tell him that I'm in the city, and that he shouldn't worry. I guess I'll just see what comes out.

I go through all the names under C without finding him and then I dial his number. I let it ring without counting the signals and I'm just about to hang up when someone on the other side finally picks up.

Hello, I say into the silence.

I picture him standing there. Maybe he was sleeping and I woke him; he's three hours behind me. I can almost feel his hair against my face.

Hello?

There's no answer but this time I hear a soft sound in the background.

Hello? I say again.

Then, finally, a fine little voice sings back to me.

Hi.

Who is this? I ask. Is that you, Michael?

He seems pleased by hearing his own name and repeats it by almost shouting it back in my ear.

Michael!

It hits me right in the gut, this weird feeling, and I have to swallow hard and pinch my leg until it stings before I can go on.

Hello, Michael. This is...

I have to swallow once again. ...Grandpa.

I don't know where all the saliva is coming from.

There's only silence on the other end, I think he might have hung up on me, but then just as I'm about to put the receiver down I hear the background noise again. First I though it was a radio but I realize now it must be the TV.

Michael, I say.

I picture him laying on the floor watching cartoons. He is laying on his stomach with the phone to his ear and it's looking way too big for his cute little hand. I think I can even make out the beeping voices from the cartoons in the background.

Listen, Michael, this is Grandpa. Is Daddy there?

Michael breathes into the receiver, tiny little breaths that I'm certain I can feel puffing on my cheek.

Daddy? he says.

Yes, is Daddy there? I ask him again.

Daddy! He yells it this time and he sounds almost annoyed for being disturbed in the middle of his cartoon.

Michael, I say, trying to sound calm, can you tell Daddy that I called? Tell him that Grandpa called.

Then the background noise is covered up again and all I hear is a scratching sound. I think he may be rolling around on the floor with the phone, and suddenly the line is cut and my last words bounce back from the empty receiver.

Be a good boy, I say and hang up.

    I stand outside the booth and I don't know where the hell I should go. From where I am streets go in all four directions and I'm thinking I could just go back and pretend I was never even gone. But that would kind of make this whole trip meaningless, and if there's one thing I don't like it is things that are meaningless.

I step back into the booth and look through the phonebook again. I look through the different sections and when I finally find one I can hardly believe it. But it's right there, printed in tiny letters next to a million others, so it must be real. I dial the number and listen to the signals go through, and, almost right away, a grown man's voice answers.

    Hello.

    Now I'm the one who doesn't say anything.

    Hello? The voice is still there.

    I try to hear something familiar about it, something I can remember, but then there's a click and the line is cut. I dial the number again and this time I don't wait for him to speak.

    It's me, I say. It's me, I repeat into the silence.

    I can't believe it, the voice finally answers back.

Even though I know it's about to happen, when a part of the past comes crashing down right behind me, it is as unexpected as a safe falling from a penthouse. I turn around and expect to see a gaping hole in the ground but instead I see a man about my own age standing there, and the only gaping hole is the one in his face.

Goddamn! Goddamn!

He's wearing a blue blazer and a hat, and in one hand he's holding a cane with a dark copper head. He keeps repeating the same word over and over again,

Goddamn! Goddamn!, like he's a tape stuck on the same loop. Finally he breaks out of it and says,

How the hell are you!, and looks me square in the face.

I don't know why but he speaks as loud as others scream.

I know damn well who he is but I don't recognize him one bit even so. I only see an old man, possibly demented, screaming out my name and holding that goddamned cane like he is about to slug someone with it. He starts across the space between us and as he gets closer something tickles my brain. Way in the very back, under many meaty folds, something stirs. I watch him hobble closer and suddenly I remember. It's all in the way he walks. Stradlater, the old bastard. I could pick that walk out in a group of a thousand.

You old bastard, I say and meet him halfway. He's thin and tall and his hand feels dry and brittle when I shake it. It might just as well have been an old stick he'd stuck out to me.

You old bastard, I say again. It wasn't yesterday.

I can tell that he is happy to see me, the way he is smiling with his whole goddamned face and all.

You old pigfucker, he says. It certainly wasn't.

And it's true, it wasn't. It was 60 years ago.

The handshake goes on and on. Stradlater doesn't let go, as if shaking forever would make up for lost time. Eventually I force my hand loose and I hear his arm snap like breaking a twig in two, but he doesn't seem to notice. He's standing all the way up close to me and I get a good look at every part of his face. I can see now that it really is him. Somewhere behind all those wrinkles and sagging skin is the once upon a time teenager Stradlater.

His hair is cut really short and it's gone completely white. I wonder what ever became of him – perhaps a military tour – but I don't feel like asking. I really don't want to talk about the past with him, what he's done, about his family and all that, I really don't. I just felt like seeing someone from my past, that's all.

He's wearing a light blue shirt and if it hadn't been for the lousy color of his skin he would have looked half alright. Underneath that smile of his there doesn't seem to be much left. I mean, he looks like he's going to keel over and die any second, and that's the reason I let him be one better than me.

You old pigfucker! he screams at me again.

We should have a million things to say, even without talking about the goddamned past, but we just stand there, staring at each other, both of our bodies swaying slightly back and forth the way two skyscrapers move in a heavy wind. Around us is busy life. People are coming and going to and from places and even though I was the one who called him up I say it mostly to break the silence.

So, you want to get a cup of coffee? Only in my head do I add, *you old son of a bitch*.

We walk across the street and into a place on the corner. We seem to be the only customers, except for an old Chinese man at the end of the counter, which goes all along the window. We get our coffee and take a seat on the other end, facing the street, so we can watch the world go by in case we can't think of anything to say to each other.

I try to take a sip of my coffee but they make it too damn hot these days and I put it down and turn my body to the side to face Stradlater. When I do I can see that he's crying. Big, crystal clear teardrops roll from his eyes and drop like aquatic bombs onto his jacket. He's not looking at me; he's not looking at anything in particular actually. Right at this moment the only thing he's doing is pushing those huge teardrops out from the corner of his eyes. I figure this is probably the reason he is so goddamn dry, what with the crying and all, but I guess it's not the right moment to mention it.

I sit in silence and wait for my coffee to cool off and for Stradlater to stop sobbing. Really, I do feel sorry for the guy. Even though I have no idea what it's all about, I do feel sorry for him. But at the same time I wish I could just disappear because this is not what I came for. I just wanted Stradlater to be the way I remembered him, an arrogant shit, just for a minute or so, to make the world seem familiar again. For a change I wanted to remember something that wasn't just in my head. That's all I really wanted.

Want to tell me what's wrong? I ask, even though I don't really want to know. Like I said, I do feel sorry for the guy but not enough to listen to some sob story. I mean, we all have our problems, right?

Stradlater dries his eyes and blows his nose in a handkerchief he pulls from his pocket. His face is swollen and all red and the little bit of color actually does him good. He looks healthier now than just a minute ago.

I can't explain it, he says, and I feel relieved.

Then it starts to rain. It's just a shower but the drops that fall are big and heavy, just like Stradlater's tears, and they fall on the window in front of us. For once I'm glad for the rain because it sort of makes us both forget about the crying.

Tell me, he says, but he doesn't continue and I don't know what it is he wants to hear.

The rain outside makes it feel like we are in a cocoon, all warm and dry, when the rest of the world is submerged under water.

Let's just sit here, ok? I say because I don't feel like talking anymore.

Ok, he says, but then after a few seconds he continues anyway.

So, how have you been?

That's the good old Stradlater right there, never listens to a goddamned word you say. He sounds better now. His nose is still running but I can tell he's back to normal, and I really don't mind shooting the crap with him a bit.

I've been pretty good, I hear myself say.

It's the same bullshit you always answer when someone asks you how you've been. I bet if you just had your foot cut off you'd *still* say the same thing.

Stradlater nods his head and I can see his reflection in the window.

Actually..., I say, and the very moment I do it's not me talking. As if being carried by a stream of water the words float out of my mouth and I don't know where they are coming from. ...I ran away from home.

When I hear it my whole body freezes into

one block of ice, then a ripple moves through me from head to toe, breaking every bone in my body. Like I said, half of the time I don't know why I do or say the things I do. I guess there's something wrong with me.

I really do want to take it back, even though it's just words and it's just Stradlater, but I can't think of anything to say that would take it away. He looks at me and for a moment I think he is about to start crying again. I decide I will get up and leave the moment he does. I don't think I can take that one more time, but then his face does a double loop and turns from shocked to amused in a second. It's not as hard as it used to be, the punch on my shoulder, not like the old Stradlater, but it still hurts.

You son of a bitch! he says. You haven't changed one bit! You almost got me there. You son of a bitch!

I smile and turn my head to the other side and I don't know what it is that I feel. My neck hurts from turning his way for too long and I hear the rain tapping the window very lightly now and I take in the smell of newly baked muffins drifting from the counter.

I'm trying to think if there's anything else before I go. I notice in the reflection of the window that both our heads move in a rhythm. I'm not sure if it's just a thing old people do; I have never noticed it before. Only very slightly do we both nod to something, perhaps the raindrops or the beat of our own slowing hearts. We get up at the same time and stop just outside the door.

Now Stradlater's voice is serious when he speaks.

It was really good seeing you again, he says, and I can tell that he really means it.

We shake hands again and this time I try to be very gentle but still his arm makes a cracking sound. Then he turns around and starts walking away. Seeing him leave makes me feel sort of crummy. Not for anything I said, but for things I didn't say. The way he was crying and all, I didn't really share anything with him. Suddenly I feel the urge to give him something of myself before we part.

Hey! I call after him. I'm 76 years old and I didn't used to be this confused. Remember? I used to be on the fencing team.

There's something in my voice that scares me. Stradlater has stopped but he's still facing the other way. If there was ever a moment I wish I could just run away or simply disappear, and not have to stand there, it would be this very moment. But I can't move. Stradlater turns around and walks back towards me and I notice he's no longer holding his cane.

Your cane, I say and I'm glad to notice he hasn't got his cane, hoping he will forget about what I just said.

But of course he doesn't and I have to stand there like some schmuck while he puts one hand on my shoulder and I see there's something in his face I have never seen before.

I stole your goddamned gloves, he says and he pats my shoulder with his hand, up and down a few times, before he goes back into the coffee shop to get his cane.

I watch his back as the door swings shut and I wait for him to come right back out. I knew it was him all along but I never could be sure. Although, right now, I couldn't care less about a lousy pair of gloves.

I wait outside for him more than a minute and I wonder what's taking him so long. The cane was right by the goddamned door and I step inside to check on him. I walk over to where we were sitting and I look around but I can't see him anywhere.

Bathroom? I ask at the counter but the guy there only shakes his head and points to a sign that says,

Sorry, no toilet.

Somehow, deep inside, I already know. Still, I look around the place again. I go over to the old Chinese man but he's sleeping with his head against the table and even though I know, I go back to the counter again and ask for him. This time I only get a shrug of the shoulders and even though I know Stradlater is gone, I wake up the Chinese man by putting my hand on his back, but it's all for no good reason. If he was ever even here he isn't anymore. He has fallen through the holes in my mind and he has vanished into thin air.

I hurry around the corner and I try to remember things as I walk. I think I'm doing pretty well, although how would I ever know what I don't remember? So, I start counting things on my fingers. Names of people I know, places I've been, years of special events, even my account number. They are all there. I look for and try to find any empty spaces, any blank spots inside, but I can't point them out, even though I know they have to be there somewhere. *Perhaps it's finally setting in*, I think to myself, and I try to count all the places Mary and I went on vacation. *Perhaps I'm finally becoming Phoebe.*

Ha, ha, ha, ha! A little pressure and the bubble bursts! I did not sanction his growth; therefore, he does not exist. What a pleasure it is to know things are still in order. Even after all this time I have not lost my touch! Now it's time for me to twist the knob to the max and end this charade.

11

The thought of it worries me but I don't know what I can do about it. Besides, I seem to remember things just fine. Perhaps Stradlater just used a back door or something because he didn't want to face me with that whole thing about the gloves and all. Like I would still care. In a way it does makes sense. I don't know what's with me these days, worrying like some goddamned girl about everything.

I walk towards the park again, not really because I want to, but that's sort of where I happen to end up. I take one of the paved paths that goes north and all around me are park workers blowing dead leaves into piles. They have these machines strapped to their backs that they use like reversible vacuum cleaners to push the leaves in front of them into big piles. Everything looks so colorful and bright in the afternoon sun and as I walk I watch it work it's way down and take on an even brighter orange, almost red color.

I pass the reservoir and stray from the path and head up over the grass towards the tennis courts. They are all empty and the gates are locked for the season. There aren't even any nets up. I really think tennis courts should always have nets up, no matter what season it is. They look so sad and pointless otherwise, the same way a ski resort looks in the middle of summer.

Not far from the tennis courts, from where I can see the corner of the high fence going around it, I find a bench and sit down. I don't see anyone else in the park, not right here, but I do hear the distant sound of honking every now and then. After a short while sitting here, thinking of nothing, I notice a woman in the distance walking in my direction. The first thing I see isn't actually her, but her hat. It's a wide-brimmed thing and it's rising up from a small pouch in the ground, followed by her face and then finally, her body all wrapped up in a herringbone coat. I watch her as she gets closer and closer, growing in size, and by the time she reaches my bench it has already become a few notches darker.

She passes me without even looking my way, stops and takes a seat on the bench next to mine. We sit like this, only a couple of feet apart, and every now and then I turn discreetly to get a look at her. She sits the same way Phoebe used to sit, very correct, her back straight as a pin and her hands resting on each leg right above her knees. The light is dimming fast now so I can't be sure, but I think she's been crying. There's a certain glow in her eyes and faint black rings line the top of her cheekbones. One thing I can be sure of though, despite the increasing darkness, is that she is very pretty.

She has long blonde hair and her face is clearly marked, almost chiseled, and her eyes are large and round. She's looking straight ahead, seemingly in a world of her own, and I'm not sure if she has even noticed me sitting where I am a few feet away. She really does catch me by surprise when she starts talking.

I bet you can't guess who I am, she says.

Her voice is small, fragile and very feminine.

It's only after those few words that her body relaxes, as if the words themselves had been stuck in her throat and now that they are out of the way she can finally breathe again. She leans back and lets out a big sigh. She lets her hands glide down from her legs and come to rest on the bench. But she still hasn't looked at me and keeps staring off into the distance.

I bet you can never guess it, she continues and lets out a small laugh that dies out just as quickly.

Suddenly a tiny flash appears on the lawn in front of us. I see that she notices it too and soon there are more flashes lighting up here and there. This seems to be enough to break whatever spell she was under and she shifts her focus from the distant world she was just in to the fireflies around us.

The evening has arrived and it won't be long before it's completely dark. Every noise is damp and I hear a hush-hush in every tree and the scraping of tiny feet in every bush. Half of the world is waking and the other half is getting ready to go to bed. I love this part of the day. It seems she does too and we sit in silence and watch the flashes appear out of nowhere before us. One by one, in no apparent order, they buzz for a second in short bursts of light before they disappear into the dark background again.

She fidgets with something in her bag. I'm only noticing now that she even has one; when she came I could swear that both her hands were empty. All around us the flashes intensify and light up another tiny area of the park. To our right, a chain reaction of tiny explosions go off in a laser like flash that pulsates forward in an arc between the trees and disappears in the distance. She sits up straight again, her eyes are fixed into the darkness. I imagine her body being very fragile under that coat, with slim wrists and an almost flat chest. A dancer's build. I don't know the first thing about her but still I can't help but feel sort of sorry for her. She seems like a young girl drowning in a too big coat. I get the feeling I should reach out and save her, that I should reach my hands deep down inside the herringbone patterned fabric and pull her out of that coat so she can breathe again.

Maybe the only reason I think this is because I hear her breathing and it's very shallow. I feel her gaze on the side of my face and I'm hoping she won't cry. I swear, if there's one thing I haven't learned it's what to do when women start to cry. Her eyes are burning my face and suddenly I can't stand it any longer. I need to reach out.

Look at the fireflies, I say.

My voice sounds old and tired.

They live only five minutes a day, and the rest is darkness. Twenty-three and some hours of nothing.

I'm sure this is not what she wants to hear, but it's all I can think of at the moment.

As if being directed by my voice, the flashes around us die down; one by one they burn out and sink back into the blackness. She has stopped fidgeting and keeps her hands motionless, still inside the bag.

I…. she says but stops herself short.

At that very moment the lamps come on and it's a sensation to see it go around the park and surround us on the outside, like one giant pearl necklace dropped from above.

I… I need to do this, she says, and I catch the flash from one of the lamps reflecting in something shiny when she pulls her hand out.

I have moved very quickly to the side and everything is now upside down. The park, the trees, the lampposts and the bench; everything is all slightly above and behind my head. I don't feel anything at first; I only hear the sharp bang of the knife as it hits the bench and then the sound of tiny feet running away from me over the gravel and into the night.

I lift my face from the grass and turn around, and for a brief moment, before the darkness swallows her up entirely, I see her legs swing back and forth like two white pendulums under the herringbone coat. Then the warmth fills my stomach.

I don't know where she came from or if she was even real, but the knife I find under the bench is so real I immediately drop it to the ground. I stay low for a while; I don't want to stand just yet. I'm trying to find the hole in my stomach to stop the bleeding. I've heard that your guts come out when you get stabbed in the stomach and you should try to hold them in and not to get any dirt on them. But it's too goddamned dark to see anything down here, so I crawl up on the bench and sit up as carefully as I can, searching my coat and body for holes in the dim electric light. I search every inch of myself but I can't find anything and as the warm wetness cools off I realize it's not blood at all, but urine. I wasn't stabbed by that crazy bitch; I have only pissed myself.

I stand up and walk towards the east side of the park. All around me I hear footsteps on the gravel path but I don't know if my mind is making things up or if there is really someone there. I also think I hear whispers, although too low for me to recognize any words, but when I stop and listen, they are gone. Despite the accident my bladder is still not quite empty so I walk in under the nearest patch of trees and relieve myself completely. The ground drinks it up and I listen to the drizzle and the whining of bicycles flashing by on the paved path that goes around the park. I know I should be happy to be alive, but honestly, right now, if I could have had my choice, I'm not sure I would have picked the piss.

I stop on the sidewalk just outside the park to think about what to do next. I'm really confused about all this. I mean, the city didn't used to be this dangerous, not even 60 years ago. There were certain places back then where you knew you shouldn't go, but I never ran into trouble, not like this anyway.

There was this one time I ran into this bloody gorilla called Maurice at this crummy hotel but that was nothing even close to getting crushed by a piece of falling metal or stabbed by a crazy woman in the park. I don't know what has happened to the city. Perhaps New York has changed too much for me to keep up with. For a moment I consider going back to Sunnyside, or even out to California to visit my son, but the feeling only lasts a few seconds. About as long as it takes for a group of young girls to come around the corner.

There are three of them, all dressed up, and they walk arm in arm, striding along in their high heels. They resemble some rare breed of furry animal as they blend giggles with laughter and pass right up close to me. I can see their perfectly white teeth flash in the night and five feet behind them floats an invisible ghost, a shadow of perfume following in their footsteps. A yellow cab drives by and the girls all put their hands up at the same time, getting the driver's attention. Then, in a fit of laughter and high pitched yips, they all cram inside the car. The door slams shut and the red glow from the brake lights goes out and as the taxi speeds away I have already forgiven New York all its faults.

There's something about the air here that caresses your insides, something that grabs you by the gut. You don't walk through the park after dark. You don't walk under building constructions. It's not too hard when you think of it. I think Sunnyside has made me soft. Spending some time in the city will help me get my wits back. Besides, the feeling I have, the one about this being the place I have to be right now, is still just as strong.

I feel sort of winded but I guess that's only normal when you've almost been killed twice in the same day, so I hail a cab and ride downtown, trying to stay awake, while keeping my eyes out for a place to stay. When I see it coming I don't have to think twice and I tell the driver to pull over.

The Roosevelt is a grand old place that sits like a throned king right on Madison Avenue. It really is a giant of a building but it's still a classy place. I mean, if buildings were trees the Roosevelt would be one of those Redwood trees out in California. It has thick red carpet on every piece of floor possible, even in the elevator, and the entrance is lit up by about a million lights. As I walk inside the doorman tilts his hat with one hand and opens the door with the other and I pull my jacket tighter around me so the stain on my pants won't show. I get a room on the 17th floor and as soon as I get out of the shower I go to bed and within a second I've fallen asleep.

There seem to be some problems. Of course, there are always problems. It seems I no longer have the same control over him. I push the right buttons, I let the ink flow and the paper roll. Next to me a small pile is forming but the words are no longer my faithful servants. They change at their own will and at first it looks as if they obey me. They dance when I say dance, I make them twirl, hop and dip just like I used to, but the moment I put the paper down and look away they dissolve and reappear in different constellations with different meaning. I push and I pull, I've tried any number of things, but I'm afraid it at best feels like tying my shoes while wearing boxing gloves.

They've changed sides and are now more his allies than mine. I suppose refugees from the same country tend to stick together. I know I have no one to blame but myself; I've left him roaming wild for too long. He's taken road upon road without me, stepping into a gigantic puzzle of roads, making him impossible to predict. All I have left now is the tiniest piece of string by which I intend to pull him out. Perhaps it's just that I'm rusty, that it's been a while since last time. Perhaps I will get into the groove of things again.

I'm trying something new. This is a long time coming, what I have just planted. I've planted a seed, a special seed of the fast growing kind. It's sprouting as we speak, shooting twiny roots into the musky soil, reaching thorny branches towards the sky. It's a bitter seed, a self-loathing seed, a seed of death. Now, I have only to sit back and let nature have its way.

12

There was a terrible noise in my head all night. I slept deeply, without waking, but the tapping just wouldn't leave me alone. It was there, in the background, all the time and when I wake up I've got a slight headache.

Like I said before, half of the time I don't even know why I do the things I do. For example, I sit up in bed trying to will my headache to go away. I do this by pretending my headache is a brightly colored paint; I usually choose yellow or blue, and I tilt my head to one side and imagine I'm emptying my head by letting the headache flow out. Anyway, as I do this I get this urge inside that I have to go somewhere again. I have no idea where but it's itching deep in the middle of me, where I can't reach to scratch, and it's just after breakfast when I leave the hotel. I don't have to walk far before it comes to me, what it is I should do. It really feels like the most natural thing in the world for me to get on the bus.

The bus is strangely empty, even from the start. The few other people that are on get off, one by one, and by the time we get there I'm all alone except for the driver. The street is stained black with oil but, had it left stains at all, it could just as easily have been sorrow. I watch as the back of the bus disappears in the distance and I'm not sure why but it makes me feel like I'm in a goddamned movie.

There's really nothing else here. The road we just came on turns on itself, becoming a snake that is eating its own tail, then goes back the way it came from. The only place I can go is through the small gate in the ragged old fence leaning a little too far to one side. This is the end of the line, and I mean that, it really is the end of the line for a lot of people. Many widowed wives and fatherless children have stood where I stand now, looking up at the stones lining the hill. They look so tiny from down here.

What things are sure in life? I can only think of one. People die. They really do. Give them long enough and they'll never let you down. I turn around and walk through the gate and start to climb the steep path.

I sure did pick one hell of a day to come to the cemetery. It's a day as gray as an old house nobody has lived in for half a century. You'd think God would have come up with some other color for gray. I mean, what good does it do anyone?

My parents are on the other side of the hill. Theirs is the first one in a semicircle of stones. Halfway up I have to stop and catch my breath. I turn around and look out over the city, at where she spreads her legs out far below. Something about her is different but I can't point to exactly what. Maybe it's only that she looks sad, with the spectrum of the hundreds of different shades of dirty bricks, along with the clouds and all, and it makes me feel a bit sad too. Right in the middle of my chest something is starting to hurt, almost like when you haven't eaten for a really long time. It's that burning sensation you get when your belly starts to eat itself. But it's not hunger that I'm feeling right now.

I keep walking and soon I make it to the top. My name is here too, and an empty space waiting to be filled. I turn into an aisle created by tall green bushes on both sides, and I keep going until I get to the very end. She's waited here a long time for me. It wasn't supposed to be like this.

I bend down and place one hand on top of her.

It's been a while, I say, because it has.

The wind rustles through the last of the leaves and I hear a squirrel rasping up a tree behind my back. I can feel it looking at me. Two hot pennies burn on my neck. I've never had to think of what to say around her; it's always come flowing so naturally.

I've been terribly busy, I say, and I know she's keeling over with laughter.

I bend down so I can be closer to the stone, closer to her, and as I lay on my side across the grass I can read myself there. Life's last address, cut in stone so it will last forever. It doesn't fill me with sorrow in any way to think of the day it will be time to go home. It's really the opposite. I have carried my name for a long time; now my name will carry me the last bit of the way.

There's this guy, a Frenchman, who walks up all the stairs, many hundreds of them, perhaps even thousands, until he gets to the top. He puts his hand on the door and it swings open; his friend has arranged it, and he steps outside. He carries a wire around his shoulder and he walks straight up to the edge and throws one end to his friend who is waiting on the other side. He has to throw it three times before his friend catches it. It's not a beautiful day; the clouds hang silent and still, not far from their heads, but it doesn't matter. There's no wind; that's what's important.

The stick is already there, or someone brings it up, I can't remember. He picks it up and walks as close to the edge as he can without going over. He pats the wire with his foot, then pushes it up and down to test it. It's a good wire. It does not move at all. He takes a deep breath and locks his eyes on the square steel door on the other side. It's not far away, but right now it seems like a million miles away, and then he steps out. The world shakes and spins, but the wire is taut and his eyes never leave the steel door. Seconds are followed by seconds but you wouldn't know because time stands still. Just as his toes reach the other side, our son lets out his first scream. For a while he is on the news all over the world. The year is 1972 and the world is never the same again.

At the cemetery it's always just one season. No matter what season it really is, at the cemetery it's always fall. Here even plants are sad. Surrounding me on all sides they hang all slumped over, like there's too much bitterness in the earth they grow from.

I clean Mary's stone by brushing off leaves and twigs that have gathered on it. Then with my finger I trace the scriptures, all the way from the beginning to the end, and then back again, until my fingertip is all red and tender. A wind begins to blow; it's tugging on my coat and pushes my hair into my face, but I'm in no rush to leave.

At first I'm surprised when I see her; not so much to see her there but the way I notice her. It's not very dramatic. It's the first warm day of summer and my parents are throwing a barbecue party. She's the daughter of a friend of the family, and there's nothing really out of the ordinary about it. We walk into each other and discover that there's something about our edges that fit. Her points fit into my cracks and my cracks smooth her points. It sounds like one helluva romance novel, but that's the only way I can describe it. We just happened to fall into the same hole. A couple of weeks later we have the names of our children picked out.

It's not fireworks; it never is with Mary. We never burn the other one up completely. We always leave something to come back to tomorrow. I ask her if she wants a drink, and she says yes. I ask her what kind, she says whatever you're making. Later, when I ask her to come with me to the beach I catch the glare in her eyes.

Certain days I look at her and see things going on inside, but I never probe. Those days she keeps the air around her so thick you couldn't push though even if you tried. On a particularly brooding day, about eight months before the aerial crossing, her nickname comes to me. I put my hand on her forehead and she closes her eyes and leans forward into my open hand.

This is what I'll call you, I say. For your face is a secret to the world.

At this time, although none of us knows it, Mary is pregnant.

I can't picture what it will be like. I imagine it will be dark and cool – in a way that doesn't bother you – but I just can't picture what it will feel like to lay there. It's too far a leap from the living to the dead. It's too wide a canyon. What was once dancing across the grass and turning a steering wheel with one hand; what was once so many things.

I sit on the ground in front of her stone and I feel blue as hell. In fact, I feel so goddamned blue I could kill myself. It's never been there before, this helpless feeling, but right now I can feel it so clearly in my chest. It's like a fast-growing weed that has rooted there and now it's sprouting and grows longer and bigger by the second. I need to be close to Mary. All I want is to be close to her. It's never felt as urgent as right now. What has this world got to offer me when all I want is right here? I claw the earth with my hand to pick up a fistful of dirt but what I get is a clump of wet leaves.

Right now I am older than anyone in my family has ever been. Older than my parents, Mary, Daniel, Phoebe, D.B. and, of course, Allie. I wonder if Daniel will ever stand in this very spot and try to see his father and mother through the dirt and the leaves? I don't want to think about it. I feel the wetness from the grass come through my pants but I don't move from where I am. I look around at the patch in front of me, the little brown patch of soil that is my life. Literally, I have one foot in the grave. Right now I am closer to death than I have ever been.

For the first time I notice the stone next to Mary's. I've never really looked around at the others but now that I sit here my eyes glance across the other stones and stop on the one next to Mary's. I don't have to lean closer to read the text, even though the stone looks to be very old. Peter Murphy. He's been laying next to her all these years and I haven't even noticed. Instantly a pinch of jealousy grabs hold of my heart. I know it doesn't make sense to feel that way. I mean, it's just a crummy gravestone. But still, the thought is there and now it won't go away. It sits there inside my head and it repeats itself over and over again. It should have been me. It should have been me. But it's been another man all along. Then a raindrop lands on my head and the same moment I start to cry.

I get the instructions at breakfast. One week it's my turn and the next it's hers. We never talk about these treasure hunts with anybody else; they are our little secrets. In the evening we lay stomach to back, telling each other of the hunt. Mary wants to hear all the details. I try to paint a picture of a particular street corner and an umbrella salesman, just before I find it. I feel her warmth through my back and I think of the next time. A hole face high in the wall behind a black pipe in Chinatown, or under a rock below the fifth oak tree in the park outside the museum. The entire island of Manhattan is our treasure chest, the tiny notes our treasures. We save them all in an old shoebox. Some are poems and some are funny messages. Some just say I love you. I still have the box. When you love someone there's so much you want to tell about them that the opposite happens.

The sky has opened up and the rain pours down over me and everything around me. The rain is like a wall that has come down and I see the bushes through a haze and soon I can't tell which is what, the oily rain or my salty tears.

I need her so much right now; I have never needed her more. It's so urgent I'm afraid my heart will snap in two and fall down into my hollow legs. I know it's ridiculous and I know I should know better, being an old man and everything, but I just can't help it. I don't care if it's childish or immature or even insane. I have to be close to Mary now or I will lose her to that man forever. I feel it as sure as I feel the rain tapping on my forehead, and just like that the thought is there.

It's a revelation appearing as a thought, and instantly it stops my crying. Despite the cold drops of rain my face feels flushed and I'm both ashamed and relieved at the same time. It's so simple. I can't understand why I haven't thought of it before. I guess I just haven't seen things clearly until now. And what is it that I see through the haze of rain when I sit on the wet grass in front of my wife's grave? I see the truth. And the truth is that I don't want to hang around anymore. I feel it in my heart; it's the right thing to do. It's the only thing to do. I'm over and done with life. What I see is Mary and me, side by side, like two sleeping sparrows.

I get up from the ground a little bit too quickly and my knees protest by making two loud gunshot pops. I'm so determined that I don't even say a proper goodbye to Mary. I just stick my cold hands in my pockets and start walking away.

I'll see you soon, I say, while my eyes are scanning the trees for the squirrel.

I can't see it anywhere and I set off down the other side of the hill. By the parking lot there's a chapel and I enter it without even knocking.

The inside of the chapel is cool and cave like. My shoes are wet and squeak against the floor and the sound echoes around the big empty room. I walk farther in and just as I begin to think that the place is empty, a man steps out from the shadows in the corner. He looks old as an owl with a long tangly beard. He's wearing thin wire glasses that rest comfortably on his meaty nose. He looks at me with his watery eyes that bulge out and for a moment I think he's just a homeless bum taking shelter from the rain, but when he speaks I know this place belongs to him.

I need to know, I say.

I stand where I am and wait until he comes back from the basement, carrying a big old book. It's the biggest book I've ever seen and it's got a leather cover and a leather band going all around it to keep it shut. The old man almost drops it down on the desk, causing a loud bang that stirs up a cloud of dust into the air. A dark and musky scent rises from inside and fills the entire room as he opens it to the first page.

He corrects his spectacles and begins by leaning into the book, searching each page methodically from left to right. While he does this he keeps mumbling something, but I can't quite make out what it is. I get an urge to ask him but I never do because I feel I shouldn't disturb him.

I've heard about trains, guns, gas, tall buildings and locking yourself in the garage with the car on, but I have never thought of this. I didn't even think it was possible until I hear it. All I know about Peter Murphy is what is written on his stone, and finally, after all this time he's decided to speak to me. The old man's nose is almost touching the paper and as I open my mouth to ask him, he starts reading. His voice is deep and purring and I step forward so I can look down at the yellowed paper. There, under the name Murphy in the year of 1932, I can look into the future.

Taken by the sea. I close my eyes and repeat it over and over in my head, until I hear the old gatekeeper close the book on Peter Murphy.

I've heard it's beautiful, he says.

I have to wait twenty minutes for the bus to arrive and as soon as it does, and I sit down, I fall asleep. I notice the world on the outside and I hear the engine, but I'm not there. When I wake up the bus speeds away from the 38th Street stop, and I rub my eyes and make myself ready to get off at the next one. I'm not sure what it is I need to do before, or if I should just go down there directly, but as the bus pulls away and I turn around and see my own reflection in a window, I know what I have to do first.

I almost can't recognize myself. My hair, even though I don't have that much to begin with, is a mess and is clumped up into some sort of ball on one side. My pants are terribly wrinkled and the hems of my jacket sleeves have chunks of dirt hanging from them. I look like I've been rolling down a wet hill or something. In any case, I look ridiculous, but even more importantly, I don't think Mary would like the look of me. I need to arrive dignified and proper, not dressed like a farmer.

I start walking back towards the hotel and along the way I keep my eyes open for a suitable place. Turns out I don't have to go far before I find it. On the corner of Lexington and 41st I find a menswear store that looks to be a distinguished place. It's called Max's Tuxedo and I step inside.

An old-fashioned doorbell jingles from above, you know, the kind they used ages ago, and without a sound a man appears from behind a curtain. It's impossible to guess his age; he's got that sort of ageless face with skin that stretches firmly around his cheeks. His hair is short cropped and steely gray, and even though his hairline is creeping to the back, I'm sure he's at least ten years younger than me. It's not hard to guess that the crown of it all is his meticulously groomed moustache. It's long and twiny and perfectly symmetrical and it ends in two soft curls. He eyes me from top to bottom where I'm standing just inside the door.

I got caught in the rain, I say, as I pat my hair down to the side.

If he thinks it's strange to come into a tuxedo shop just like that to buy a change of clothes, he sure doesn't show it. He acts as if it was the most natural thing in the world, as if he got two or three customers like me every single day.

Very well, Sir, do come in, he says and extends his arm towards me.

At first I think he wants to shake hands but when I get closer I realize it's my coat he wants. I hand it over and watch him disappear with it behind a curtain, the same way you would carry out a dead dog. I take a seat in a leather armchair and wait for him to return.

I look around the room and all around me are rows and rows of black tuxedos hanging from cherry wood walls. It's the same when he comes back; he doesn't make a sound. Suddenly he's just standing there next to me.

I have to tell you, I say and pause.

He tags on directly where I leave off – he would make an excellent butler – and he says,

Max, and nods towards the sign above the store front.

I have to tell you, Max, I say as I look him straight in the eyes, I need something for a funeral.

Max asks me to stand up and, while I do, he walks once around me before he dives into the wall racks. He moves in and out, very smoothly, down to the very end of the wall, and when he returns he's holding a black suit in his hands.

I believe this is for you, Sir, he says.

The changing room is made from a thick red velvet drape that is hung from the ceiling in the shape of a square. I sit down on the stool inside and start untying my shoes. Max hangs the suit on a hook, closes the drapes behind him and leaves me alone. There's a light in the ceiling, a mirror in one corner and the stool I'm sitting on, but apart from that and the red velvet cocoon that's embracing me, it's empty.

I start pulling my pants down but I only get halfway before I catch myself in the mirror. An old man with his hair clumsily folded to one side is looking back at me. His bones are sticking out from underneath his sagging skin and his forehead is scrunched up in deep brooding folds. *I'm doing the right thing*, I tell myself. *Daniel will understand.*

Everything alright, Sir? The voice from outside sounds muffled and far away.

I pull my pants up and start tying my shoes.

Sir? I hear Max's voice again, just as I pull the drapes to the side.

I'll take it, I say and hand it to him.

When I get to the desk my coat is already hanging from the hat rack beside the door. I touch it and it's still warm. Then something strange happens. As Max hands me my bag he intentionally lets his hand remain on mine for an extra second. I mean, I can tell it's intentional by the way he does it. Besides, it wouldn't be like him to do something like that; it doesn't fit with his character, and that's why I'm surprised.

Sir, if I may say something.

Even though he keeps his eyes directed at me he doesn't seem to actually see me. It's more as if he's looking into the distance. I even think I see the faintest of smiles twinkle under his moustache as he speaks.

There's no reason to be alive just for the sake of it.

And that's it. As soon as he's done he lets his hand fall from mine and his gaze goes back to normal again. He looks me in the eyes and he's now the same proper man I met when I first stepped into the store. I'm sure he knows I never tried the suit on but this Max would never mention it. I don't know what to make of it, I really don't want to start pulling on that thread. I have things I must do.

Goodbye, I say, and the jingle from above the door remains in my head for several blocks.

13

I stop by my room quickly to change clothes but I don't bother to shower since I will get wet anyway. I just comb my hair and get into my new suit, and wouldn't you know, Max was right; it fits just perfectly.

I take a cab to Battery Park but get off at ground zero and walk the last bit of the way. I feel good in my new suit; I can't even remember the last time I wore one. They don't come often in your life, the times you wear a new suit, I mean. You know when you do that it's either someone's best day or their worst day. And the very last time you wear one you won't even notice it. Except for the exceptions. Like right now.

These are the same waters, where the Hudson meets the East River, where Peter Murphy was taken by the sea. He worked at the South Seaport, on the ferry going across to Staten Island, and one day he simply disappeared from the deck.

I pick a spot on the most southern tip of Manhattan and lean on the railing between me and the water. A mother passes behind my back with her child in a stroller and I feel like telling her what a nice day it is. Because it really is. The sky has opened up and is blue the same way a baby's eyes are blue, and seagulls fly up and down from the water, carrying bits of food in their beaks. Soon enough you will have to come as far as seeing the point of it all. Everybody has to. And then you simply choose.

A park worker passes by behind my back in a golf car. He's talking on a radio and when I see him turn around the corner I swing one leg over the railing, followed by the other. I balance on the small ledge and it I really does feel good in my new suit, and then I fall forward. They say it's beautiful.

The water is very cold and dark, it's color is almost steel blue. Foam has formed on the surface and I see it appear in tiny clouds around my head for a few seconds, before it disappears away from me in the current. At first I kick my legs and move my arms to stay up, without realizing what I'm doing. Then, as soon as I do, I make myself relax and try to put my hands in my suit pockets only to realize they are still stitched together. Instead I shove them into my pants pockets and I lean back and wait for it to happen. The current is pulling me out and then back, sort of in a circle. I see the ledge and the tip of the trees in the park above, then part of New Jersey in the distance, and then open water. I go around and around and, for some reason, before I go under, I take a deep breath.

At first I don't recognize her. I only see a woman with long red hair. She's at the bottom and I fall towards her slowly. She seems to be waiting for someone and when I land on the packed mud I see that it's Molly.

Allie died a long time ago and the thing about him was that you had to love him. I'm not kidding, everyone did. Even though he tried to latch on when we were riding our bikes down to the old cemetery, or going treasure hunting behind Leeman's Cove and was left behind, he never once got sore. It's true, I don't think I ever saw Allie sore once. Even though he was the youngest, in many ways he was the most grown up of all of us.

When he died, everything changed. Phoebe was too small to remember but my mother and father changed a lot. I remember my mother getting these nervous spells for no apparent reason, and my father spent more time in the office, even more than he had before. I never really knew about D.B., how he felt and all. He went away to college right after and then he moved out to California and wrote that story about the goldfish. It was only when they sent his things out to New York that I found out how hard it had been for him. I can't ever recall seeing D.B. cry, not once, even though, of all of us, he was the one who took Allie's death the hardest.

When I talk to him the TV shows fires raging in the hills of California. He tells me he can see plumes of black smoke from his kitchen window. He sounds tired.

It's early morning Pacific time. My mother calls me before noon. It's Tuesday and it's November. The doctor tells us 05:02. That means I have just finished teaching my first class. The note says, **Call your mother.** She doesn't say the words, not right away; she's still hoping someone's made a mistake.

Your father is flying out there right now.

Her voice echoes in the receiver as if we were a million miles away from each other.

You need to come home, she says.

A big gap is missing from inside myself. A space has opened up and it won't close back together. It sits right next to other open spaces and no matter what I try it won't close up. I rush over there as fast as I can. On my way I wonder if this is how life is supposed to be. You start out whole and end up like a goddamned Swiss cheese.

Everything is so still under water. I have been submerged into a slow motion world where even my thoughts take longer to bridge the gap in my head. I can't tell where the light is coming from but I see Molly clearly as she sidles up next to me. Her silvery tail glimmers in the muddy water stirred from the bottom. Tiny bubbles escape my nose and race to the surface in front of my face. Molly extends her arm around my back and pinches my neck lightly, and when she does I feel warm all the way into my bones.

We put the boxes in my old room. In there it smells just the way it did ten years ago, as if the air has been trapped in a bottle all this time. I start with the one on top and continue with the next, working my way down to the bottom of each one. I try to concentrate on the things in the boxes and not on my mother's crying. One after another I pick things up and hold them against my face, before I put them to the side. I can't begin to tell you what a crummy feeling it is when you see it like this, seven boxes for one whole life.

I get to the last box and it's too heavy to move so instead I sit down on the floor right next to it. Inside are stacks of notebooks and I pick up the first one and start reading. Page after page are filled with words, words that were my brother's life.

My eyes hurt and the street below has turned silent. My parents have closed the door to their room and I can no longer hear my mother's sobs. The box is empty and I'm filled to the brim with my brother's thoughts and ideas. I look around the room and in a blur I see my red hunting cap hanging from the side of my bed and, one by one, tears wet the pile of notebooks in my lap. Death by overdose. Three little words that changed our lives.

It's a sunny day with a clear blue sky. It's so blue the air is vibrating when you look at the horizon. The sun hits Molly's enormous flow of hair as she steps into the minimal back seat, leaving the front to me, and lights up her head like it was a ball of fire. I fold the seat back and sit down and almost immediately she playfully pinches my neck. Usually that sort of thing would drive me crazy but now it feels alright.

Molly is one of those Hollywood nymphs that looks designed to lay around the pool all day and attend fancy cocktail parties at night. She can pinch my neck all she wants.

D.B. has put the top down and he roars the car out of the parking lot and continues all the way up on the Pacific Coast Highway without taking his foot from the accelerator. The car is brand new and it howls and growls from under the hood but stays flat as an iron on the road. Molly's hair stands straight out the back in a plume of red, resembling a crazy Medusa on top of a cliff. I look at her in the mirror and notice her lips are perfectly red and slightly parted. D.B. turns to me and grins. It's a wolfy smile that lasts only a second, but it's a second that lasts forever. He squeezes the steering wheel tight with his leather gloved hands and he flies us down the coast in a thin line, straight as a silver arrow, between the roaring Pacific and the jagged rocks.

A few days after discovering the last notebook, I receive a letter. It's from Molly. *I know your brother*, it starts, then, right away, she corrects herself. *I knew him.* Before I can even continue I picture her sitting there. She's at her kitchen table, smoking a cigarette while writing me this letter. Her elbow is resting on the old wax cloth and one of her worn sandals dangles loosely from her heel. Outside, in the warm evening air, the night crickets sing. *I thought you ought to know what happened to your brother.* I can almost smell the scent of her cigarette on the paper. *What kind of life he was living,* she continues. *He talked a lot about you, about his brother out in that goddamned New York City. He thought the world of you, you know. That's why I thought you should know what happened.* Her red locks fall forward as she leans into the letter, holding the end of the cigarette towards the open window. *I guess you know by now that D.B. had a drug problem. He had it for quite some time.* The smoke eases through the crack and disappears into the night without a sound. *I don't know how much you know about drugs, but they took away parts of your brother that were parts of himself. Sometimes it was so bad he didn't even recognize me.*

I see it in front of my eyes, the way Molly tells it, the image of D.B. stumbling through the door late one night. His eyes are all bloodshot and his shirt a crumpled mess. His hair stands on end and a layer of sweat covers his pale face. As he walks though the door he stops because he does not recognize the woman sitting in the chair just inside. *He tried many times to get help, went to clinics and doctors, but after a few weeks hanging out with the same crowd he fell back into it again.* Towards the end the letter gets messier, as if the person writing is in a hurry to finish. It ends, *Please don't blame yourself. Molly.*

There's some commotion on the surface but I can't be bothered with it right now. I am here and that's happening someplace else. Molly notices it too, she looks up and lets go of my neck. As she does my body at once becomes cold and I start to shake. Bubbles no longer come from my nose and I see Molly clearly in front of me. She swims around me once and then stops with her face one inch from mine. She looks worried. Her lips are perfectly red and slightly parted and for a moment I think she is about to kiss me. Then everything moves fast, faster than it should under water. I see the mud floor move away from me quickly and all I can really think of is why Molly is pulling my hair so hard.

It's laying on the bottom of the last box. I don't see it at first because it has slipped under one of the cardboard flaps. Only a tiny corner of it is visible and it's pure luck that I happen to spot it. I pull it out and let it rest in my open palm. It's an ordinary notebook, a spiral bound cheap thing bought from some supermarket, and I'm afraid to open it; I'm afraid because it's the last one.

I sit for a long time and try to imagine what is written in it by looking at the five words scribbled on the cover. I hold it like that in my palm, seemingly for many hours, until I hear the garbage trucks gasp from the street below. Then I know it's morning.

In the end I never do open the notebook. I put it back under the flap and cover it carefully with the rest of them. I don't want things to ever change. I want to keep them as they are. I figure as long as I don't open that notebook, one day D.B. will be picking me up in his new car, and Molly will be in the back seat, playfully pinching my neck and we'll fly across the highway on his silver arrow, his face grinning at me in the afternoon sun. The bathroom floor in a cheap motel on Sunset doesn't matter. What matters is the sun, the car, the wind in our faces, Molly's red hair, my brother's leather gloves and his grin. That and those five little words.

14

M r. C! Mr. C!

The words are so loud in my ear that they make my head hurt. Everything around me is yellow and when I try to speak a thick fluid pours from my mouth instead of words. I feel myself slide back into the water and it's warm and pleasant, but only for a second. The next thing I know I'm back in the yellow and the same voice is piercing my brain

Mr. C! Mr. C!

Why can't they just let me sleep in peace?

I hear a siren from far away and it sounds much nicer than the voice in my ear. I focus on the metallic wailing and try to move towards it, away from the voice, but I can't find my arms and legs. I want to lift them but I don't know where to start.

I can't hear the siren anymore, only the sound of someone breathing hard into my ear. Then there's a pressure around my chest and I vomit again. The fluid is nice and warm on my stomach and I feel like I'm floating up in the air and soaring there for a moment. Then I'm back down laying on my back. Something crawls over my face from the side, a giant crab perhaps, but it couldn't be a crab because it's hairy. It's some kind of black animal and it sits right over my face and I can feel it smelling of garlic. The last thing I hear before everything goes black, but now from a distance, is that same voice, still calling me.

Mr. C! Mr. C!

What kind of nonsense is this? Are there holes in this world I know nothing about? Back doors from other stories, or even from other worlds? But it can't be. It mustn't be. It's even impossible. This must simply be an act of pure chance that happened to intervene with my creation. Just like a tree falling in the forest, crushing a hunter about to pull the trigger on a deer. Sometimes these things happen and you can't predict them anymore than you can predict lightning. I will pick up my pen and get back in the saddle.

The soup is very warm and very sour. My tongue cringes every time the old lady pours it into my mouth with a ceramic spoon. She doesn't say anything to me; she simply moves the spoon from the bowl to my mouth and back to the bowl again. Her hair is gray and it's bound together at the top of her head in a bun that spirals upwards, narrower and narrower, in the shape of a tepee. As I open my mouth to receive another spoonful I catch a glance of the room behind her and see that there's no other furniture, no chairs and no table, except for the mattress I'm laying on. The old lady is sitting cross legged next to me, right on the floor. She keeps the bowl in her lap and every time she feeds me a spoonful I get another look around the room.

I notice two windows up by the ceiling and in front of one of them is a thin wired birdcage hanging from the roof. Two yellow finches are looking at me in silence from inside. I hear a distant chatter from somewhere above and the finches seem frightened by my presence. When I've finished most of the soup the old lady leaves me without a word. I'm covered in many blankets, all the way up to my nose, and I shiver for a moment before I close my eyes and fall asleep.

When I wake up Charlie is sitting on the floor under one of the windows and I see now that we are below street level. A forest of legs is walking by on the outside and I wonder what she is doing here. Is this part of a dream? It must be. She spots me looking at her and comes over and sits down next to me, cross legged, just like the old woman.

She places one hand on my forehead and now I know it's not a dream.

Mr. C, how are you feeling?

I remember Charlie used to like the old classics. *The Last of the Mohicans, Seven Leagues Under the Sea, The Call of the Wild*, and many others. She was quiet and very polite and she always submitted her papers on time.

You fell in the water, Mr. C.

She removes her hand and starts pulling on the covers. She's trying to get them even higher up and when she's satisfied she tucks them in tight around my neck.

You are lucky I saw you.

I try to recall what her special project was about but I can't seem to remember it right now.

You just rest for a while, Mr. C, Charlie says and leaves me alone once again.

The covers piled high on top of my chest weighs about a ton and I fold half of them down so that I can breathe. Immediately it feels better. I feel my bladder pressing against my stomach and I squeeze out from under the covers and sit up. For the first time since I woke up I realize I'm totally naked. I look around the room to see if my clothes are anywhere near but I can't see them and creep back in bed again, unsure of what to do. But after only five minutes it hurts too much and I just can't hold it any longer so I get up again. The floor is nice and warm under my feet and I use one of the blankets to cover myself. I wrap it around my waist and walk through the same door Charlie and the old woman disappeared through.

In the stairwell there are many things. I spot a couple of bikes, boxes filled with old magazines, what looks to be sacks of rice and a yellow kayak leaning against the wall. Out here the floor is cold and I move as quickly as I can over each step up to the first floor. I don't know where to go. I see the street through the front door and I see an Asian couple on their way up the steps. I turn around and hurry back down because I don't want them to see me, not like this anyway, and I sneak behind the kayak and relieve myself in an empty paint jar.

Just as I get back into bed, Charlie comes through the door again. She sits down next to me and puts one hand on my forehead. It feels cool and soft against my skin.

I'll tell Grandma to bring you some more soup, she says and her voice no longer sounds sharp in my ears.

I tell her that I'm fine and ask her if she can please bring me my clothes, and to thank her grandmother for the soup, but I couldn't possibly eat any more of it right now. She leaves and returns after five minutes with my suit dried and neatly folded in a pile.

Thank you, Charlie, I say when I'm finished

getting dressed and she turns around again from facing the corner.

I'm not sure what happened. I think I reached for something and fell.

She doesn't say anything and in some peculiar way I don't want to look at her. I can feel her eyes on me but I keep mine on the finches in their cage, and they in turn look at Charlie. Together we form a perfect triangle of attention.

Mr. C, she finally says and smiles at me, I'm just glad you are ok.

I'm not sure if it's the same day or if Battery Park happened yesterday, but I think it's still the same day. We leave the house and enter a street I can't say I recognize, but I know it's somewhere in Chinatown. The sky is overcast and I think it must have been another day after all. I tried to leave without her but Charlie insists on walking with me. I still feel tired and cold, all the way deep inside my bones, and I don't want to argue with her after what she and her grandmother have done for me. I mean, how could they have known?

After only a block or so I feel too tired to walk so I hail a cab and Charlie gets in right behind me. She rides with me up to the Roosevelt and follows me through the lobby and up in the elevator, then she walks with me down the corridor all the way to my room. All this time we hardly say a word to each other; we simply walk side by side. I'm too tired to even be bothered. When we get to my door I open it and with my hand still on the handle I turn around and face her.

Thank you, Charlie, I say, for everything.

Surprisingly she leaves without a word and I watch her walk down the winding stretch of corridor, one finger on her left hand dragging along the wall, tracing the pattern on the wallpaper.

Who is she, the one who seems to know him so well? Where does she come from? I know I shouldn't let my curiosity have its way like this, but I need to know. I need to know what that world is like. I know what I should do. I should stay focused and apply the right pressure to each key, one after the other, and the tiny arm will hit, hit and hit, and before long my deed of freedom will roll out. But I must follow them for a little while, just for a little while. I must, so I can see another fragment of that world. After all, I am the cat and he the mouse; what harm could a bit of playing around do? He has tormented me for years. I have made up my mind. I will stay sharp and pull the plug when I have to. Not a second later.

It does bother me that I don't know how much he knows. What parts of him are still the same? Do they create life all by themselves? Are they flesh and blood like you and I? Can they even die? I have to find out and I think she will help me. Either way, I can't make him go away just like that. There's no clear path to where he is now. I can make buildings tumble but I can't tumble them exactly where I want. It's like he has some sort of shield that protects him. I really have to work it as a chess board. One piece, five steps ahead. Whatever I plan will be carried out fives steps ahead.

I'm not yet sure if she's a spawn of his mind – a creation in the creation so to speak – or if she's a version of reality. But then, of course, the million dollar question remains. How could she possibly be real when he's not? No interaction is allowed; more so, it's not even possible. They all come from here, from these very fingers.

These days the tips of my fingers don't bother me anymore, they are calloused and numb, but my back still aches after each day. It's a dreary job, at best, which I make bearable by imagining. When I let my imagination go I see myself as a knight; it's ridiculous but it's true. I'm a knight in shining armor on a dark bridge, casting giant letters made out of orange sized chunks of steel, with edges sharpened into razorblades. I throw and I throw against the forces of evil until dawn breaks and I can finally rest.

I throw and I throw and I nudge and I squeeze her through the door.

When we get to my door I open it and with my hand still on the handle I turn around and face her.

Thank you, Charlie, I say, for everything. Charlie turns to look at me and for a while none of us moves, then I give in and nod my head slightly.

As soon as we get in I lay down on the bed and she takes a seat in the chair by the window. It's later in the day when I wake up and she is still sitting there, reading a book. I don't know where she got it from because I didn't bring any, but nevertheless, she sits there reading one. I go to the bathroom and splash some water in my face and I'm starting to feel a bit better. I'm not cold anymore, and when I look in the mirror I notice I have gotten my color back. My face looks almost tanned against my bright white shirt. The old lady did a marvelous job on both of us.

In the restaurant on the ground floor I order a club sandwich and Charlie orders a shrimp cocktail.

This is a real classy place, Mr. C.; everyone that works here wears a uniform.

We are waiting for our drinks to arrive and she keeps looking around to take the whole place in.

I bet even the chef wears one.

Her hair is jet black and it's cut straight all around, ending just above her eyebrows in a sort of Asian-style pageboy. She seems more lively now than from when I remember her.

The people in here probably look at us and think it's a family gathering.

She squints her eyes when she speaks.

Grandfather and adopted granddaughter, and she lets out a giggle.

I turn and look around. I cannot recall ever being here before. There are only a few other guests in the restaurant at this hour of the day; an old couple at a table near the door that sit so close together you'd think they share the same body and a man sitting by himself with his back to us so I can't see his face at all. He sits sort of hunched over forward, working on his dish with great energy. I've known before, of course I've known, it's just that right now it stands out more than it has in the past, that everybody around us all have life in them. They have families, relatives, jobs, trips, memories, old cabins, fishing gear, a sore toe, blisters, hopes and regrets. I want to tell her about it but I don't know how to start. It doesn't make any sense to even explain why she found me in the water. Then our food arrives and I don't have to think about what to say anymore.

Charlie watches me from across the table. I pick up my sandwich with both hands and take a bite. She is different from when she was in my class, different from this morning even. She picks up a shrimp with two fingers, dips it in the sauce, bends her head back and drops the shrimp into her mouth.

Did you know, she says and swallows eagerly, that this place is owned by Pakistan?

I try to remember what row she sat in and what grade I gave her, but I just can't retrieve it. She continues to fill her mouth with shrimp in a never ending movement between her hand and cup.

The Roosevelt Hotel, an American institution, with the Roosevelt Grill, she says as she sweeps her hand in a semicircle, where Guy Lombardo performed 'Auld Lang Syne' for the first time. Did you know that it is owned by the Pakistan International Airline?

I take a sip of water but it's as if I've had enough of water for a while and I let it flow back into my glass.

That's gross, Mr. C. No offense, but that's gross, Charlie says and drops yet another shrimp into her mouth.

She was one of several hundred students. Still, I'd like to remember what she wrote. Once, right before summer, she had been away for several weeks and when she came back it was the last week of school. I remember I wrote her a list of things to catch up on until the next semester. I could have flunked her but I didn't want to. I don't remember what I wrote on that list but I remember I thought she looked very pale and skinny and I felt sorry for her.

I mean, what's next? Selling the Statue of Liberty to Argentina? she asks.

I smile at her, not for what she is saying or for the way she is dropping shrimp after shrimp into her mouth, but for what she's making me remember.

When we're done I suggest we go for a walk. I don't know what Charlie's plans are, but I'd like her to leave me alone now. We walk west, side by side, without talking. It seems as soon as we walk neither of us has anything to say. She's shorter than me, naturally, and perhaps it's her height that gives her that stubborn look. I can't remember her looking that way in the past. I don't know where we are heading; I just want to find a moment and a place where I can turn around and leave. It's like going through a lot of trouble to get to a remote spot just so you can get rid of a dog you don't like. It's not really that I dislike her all that much; I just want to get on with things. I feel I don't have that much time and I need to hurry up before it's too late.

After a couple of blocks we cross 5th Avenue and turn south. We still don't speak and a few more blocks down, on the corner of 31st Street, I stop and look up at my old lamp. It's still there, after all this time. The rest of the offices look different now, somehow cleaner, less cluttered with things. I can picture myself standing on the sidewalk from up there, the way I used to look out that window so many times. I can even hear the ticking of the old radiator in the winter. There was a time when I knew ever flake of paint and every bolt on the facade across the street, every shirt the man in the third floor apartment owned and the pattern on the back of every pigeon sitting on the crest of the roof.

You need to go home, I say to Charlie, still keeping my eyes on my old light.

Her answer comes directly, as if she'd been waiting all this time for me to go first.

I saw you, Mr. C, she says. I saw you jump.

15

The Russian deli isn't here anymore. I had guessed it wouldn't be, but I didn't know. Instead we go to the coffee shop that is now where the deli used to be. Back then I went once a week, always on Thursdays. That's when they served the red beet soup. I remember the woman behind the counter; her name was Bertha. Every time I walked in she polished the marble counter with an old washcloth, no matter what time I came in. Even as I walked past in the evenings she was there, leaning forward, grinding the marble down with her that piece of cloth. I don't know what happened to the place, or to Bertha. Perhaps she finally polished her way through the hard Italian rock, threw her arms up in a victory gesture, and walked straight out and never looked back.

The coffee shop now is just another coffee shop and we take our cups and sit by a table near the door.

Charlie, I say, but I don't continue.

My coffee is too hot to drink, even to hold, and I let it stand on the table in front of me.

Charlie, I start again, but still I say nothing more.

Charlie looks at me from across the table. Her eyes are raven like and sharp and I look away. Two tables from us sits a couple and their baby. The man is biting down on a huge sandwich while the woman is holding the baby. She's holding it with its back to her and she is trying to get it to stand on her knees. The baby is trying and trying and the mother gives it balance by holding onto it's tiny hands, but the baby's legs are just too weak and keep collapsing, over and over.

I try my coffee again but it's still too hot and I burn my upper lip. The silence is a screen between us. Behind the couple I see a pretty girl sitting next to a guy in a blue shirt. I can't see his face because he has his back to me, but the girl is very pretty with long, wavy hair. The baby keeps trying to stand without making it and as the baby's leg kicks out it hit the table and a pair of sunglasses falls to the floor. I see them laying between the two tables. They look so very sad where they are, so vulnerable in the wide open space, and finally I do think of something to say.

Did you ever finish the list I gave you that summer?

I look at her, then at the sunglasses on the floor, then at the struggling baby, then back at Charlie. She has already finished her coffee even though hers was as warm as mine. She doesn't answer my question and I think for a moment that she hasn't heard me.

You remember, the paper? I say.

Without answering me she pushes a single tear from the corner of her eye. It glides all the way down her cheek and comes to a halt under her chin. For a couple of seconds it hangs there, like a brilliant pearl, and it doesn't fall until Charlie opens her mouth.

I was in love with you, she says, and the tear finally drops and lands with a dull plop in her empty coffee cup.

The baby looks as if it will start to cry any second now but the mother refuses to give up and keeps trying to get it to balance. Mary used to joke about it, how the students would fall in love with me, how when she was young she had fallen in love with her teacher. There's only the one tear and somehow I think it would be easier if there had been more.

Someone dropped sunglasses on the floor, I say, and look at them.

Charlie doesn't take her eyes off me when she speaks.

I won't leave you, she says. I will stay with you until you promise you won't do that again.

The man in the blue shirt gets up and goes over to the counter. His foot misses the sunglasses by a couple of inches and I feel my heart skip a beat.

If you try to get rid of me I will scream rape.

I see the man come back with a handful of napkins.

I'm not kidding, she says. You know I'll do it.

I see his foot in slow motion as it lands on the sunglasses and even Charlie turns around at the sound of snapping plastic and crushed glass. I sigh deeply and look at her. There is a triumphant smile on her face. As she leans forward and rests her elbows on the table I see that she looks like one of those Japanese cats with waving arms. I could say it and get it over with. Right now, I could promise her and be on my way. But all I do is sigh and pick up my cup and blow away the steam from the top. The damn thing is still too warm to drink and I have to put it down again and finally I look into her eyes.

How do you do it? I ask, because I really would like to know.

Charlie insists we go to the secondhand store across the street. The girl behind the counter is wearing randomly selected pieces from the flooded hangers. She is a collage of patterns and different material, and so is the store. It's filled to the brim with racks of washed out t-shirts with faded prints, old navy jackets with gold stripes, and in the back a row of old cowboy boots.

I love these places, Charlie says. I love the smell of old things she says and buries her head in a pile of knitted sweaters.

As soon as they start crying I don't know what to do. At the moment I'm being held hostage by a 26-year-old girl.

While Charlie tries on fur hats in front of the mirror I have nothing to do but to walk over to the row of cowboy boots. They smell of leather and sweat rubbed together over the years, so I guess these boots really do come from genuine cowboys.

Do you like it? Charlie asks behind me.

I turn around and look at her. She has on a Russian fur hat that makes her look like an eskimo.

It makes you look taller, I say, not trying to sound either angry or the opposite.

Charlie pokes her tongue out at me and walks back to the hats. I need to use the restroom and as the girl points me downstairs I notice how Charlie watches me, from the corner of her eye, every step I take.

The bottom floor looks just like the main floor; it's also filled with racks and tables full of clothes, and I find the bathroom in the very back. When I'm done I don't hurry directly back up, instead I browse along the aisles of clothes and stop in front of a row with long coats. I can see the bottom of the stairs from where I stand and it's her ankles I see first. Quickly I step in between the hangers and wrap myself in a coat. I try not to breathe and I listen to any steps coming closer, but I can't hear a goddamned thing surrounded as I am by all the coats. Each minute feels like five and soon enough I start to sweat. There's also something in the coat brushing up against my face that irritates my nose. It's some sort of old cologne or something and my nose starts itching. I mean, it starts itching real bad. Drops of sweat have formed on my forehead and I have to bite down on my lip to keep myself from sneezing. It must be ten minutes now. At least ten minutes. I make up my mind to wait another five but at that same moment a sneeze explodes from my nose and there's nothing I can do about it. As if that wasn't enough, I lose my balance and fall out from between the coats and land in a pile of coats on the floor.

Charlie is standing right there. She looks down at me with a face impossible to read and all she says is,

You're not at all as I imagined, Mr. C.

She is waiting for me by the counter. She is wearing the hat so I guess she must have bought it. For a second I'm thinking I could run around the corner and get into a cab real quick and tell the driver to speed away before she can catch up to me, but I'm not sure I'm fast enough. Not with all the madcap stuff I've been through lately. And that's when I see it. If I could take it in my hand and measure it on a golden scale, this single moment, it would be priceless. Behind Charlie, on a shelf above the register, between a Sgt. Pepper's album and a ceramic bear with a rainbow-striped belly, is a red hunting hat. When I hold it in my hand I see that it's not exactly the same as the one I used to have but pretty damn close. This one has a small leather patch in the front with the word Wolfpack stitched on it. The inside of the ear flaps have fluffy white lining, where my old hat had fluff in a more yellowish tone, but other than that they are the same. I've never seen one like it since my old one and I wonder if this is some sort of omen.

I'll take it, I say to the rag doll girl and I feel Charlie's breath against my neck.

Copycat, she whispers.

When I wake up and she's there. Always in that same chair, although this time she's not reading, but sleeping. She looks very peaceful with her legs pulled in under her and the blanket that's wrapped around her body has fallen down from her one shoulder. I'm guessing it's around 8 o'clock and I walk across the room to the bathroom and close the door as quietly as I can. When I'm done I don't flush; instead I sneak out and carefully grab the shoes from under my bed and open the door.

Good morning, a tired voice says from behind me.

I'll meet you in the breakfast room, is what I want to say, but there has to be a better way. I close the door while I wait for her to get ready.

On the way down I look at our reflections in the elevator mirror. The two of us standing side by side; we look like we came straight out of a comic book. My old face with its deep cut lines, in the black funeral suit, gives me a haggard look. Charlie with her white blouse, exact trimmed hair and spotless skin that sparkles, looks animated in a way. I'm looking deep into my own eyes, at the reflection of the reflection, another one of me, and another, when Charlie speaks.

I dreamt about you, she says.

The elevator hums and my reflection isn't backing off.

Me too, I say without really thinking. I had the tapping dream again.

Now Charlie's reflection is looking at me as well.

You were dead, she says. Dead at the bottom of a cliff.

When I hear that I smile. I can't help it and

it's not at all because it's funny. I really don't want to upset her but something inside me pulls on a string and it makes me smile. It's only a real quick smile and it's over in a second. I don't think she even notices.

It was just a dream, I say and put a comforting hand on her shoulder as we step out of the elevator.

We take a cab over to the park and in the corner of my eye I watch her yawn. My guardian angel. I think she will tire soon. Another night in the chair and I should be free. Another night and I will be on my way again. The driver just keeps going and neither of us says anything. Not until we're all the way over on Amsterdam Avenue do I tell him to stop. I really don't mind it, going way over here. I've always found that this particular area reminds me of San Francisco. I don't know why, maybe it's the way the avenues run sort of slantwise up a hill, over something large bulging up from the underground. It's the only place in the city that does that, reminds me of San Francisco, I mean.

We walk east and by now I'm used to the silence. Silence between two people is different than the silence you make by yourself, but it still doesn't bother me. As we get closer I see it towering up in the distance. It's actually pretty strange but I always seem to end up there. No matter where I go, eventually I always end up in Central Park. It must be the center of my universe or something.

The west side of the park has more space and the trees here are taller. They are the forefathers to all the other trees. Charlie yawns again and I try to pick up the pace. I stray from the paved path and set out under the shadowing trunks. I step across the earthy ground covered in leaves and I feel it give slightly under my weight. Even though I see Central Park West to my right and I hear the sounds of the city, I can't help but think of myself as an adventurer. I am making my way through a frontier, stepping where no man has stepped before.

Wait up, Charlie calls from behind, and I try to make my steps even bigger.

The trees stand silent and steady but it's obvious that they know what's going on. At the end of the earthen patch I find the road blocked by a thin wire fence. I swing my leg over to the other side but as I follow with the next I get caught on something and I hear my pants rip in the back. It's just below my left back pocket and when I stick my finger through the hole I can feel my hairy leg. I press on it and it has the consistency of a mushroom.

I still have a little distance on her; I don't care about the hole and continue walking. One foot in front of the other, air moving in and out of my lungs. Then, without warning, it all falls apart. From out of nowhere, the same black animal crawls into my vision, starting from the corner of my eye. It's not something from the park, it's from inside my head. Between its rough black fibers I see a bench up ahead and I aim for it. A tingle rises from the base of my spine and I don't know if I can make it, but I clamp my teeth together and, like an airplane trying to get back to home base, I set out to cross the ocean. It's not far, only a couple of yards, only a few feet perhaps, but the black animal is now covering most of my face. I want to throw out piece after piece into the dark blue water to lower the weight. I hear my engine sputter and I try everything I can to make the fuel last all the way home when suddenly I feel Charlie's arm under mine.

New York has changed a lot throughout my lifetime but Central Park has remained pretty much the same. It's possible that I have sat on this bench before but if I have I don't remember it. It's placed right under one of the tallest trees I've ever seen and when I look up from where I'm laying on my side, I can hardly see its crown way up there in the sky. My head is resting in Charlie's lap and she has one hand placed on my forehead again, and the other on my back. In front of me, way out on the end of the bench, I see a half-eaten sandwich in an open wrapping. The black animal is gone and only a slight dizziness remains, but I stay where I am for now. The sun is out and warm rays land on my right cheek as I watch a parade of ants marching towards the sandwich. One by one, in a long row, they climb up from the ground on one of the steel legs, following each other in a nearly perfect line. I watch as the first ant comes over the bend and drops down on the sitting board. The other ones follow right after in the first one's footsteps and when they get to the sandwich they stop for a second, open their scissor like jaws, and clamp down on the bread. They take one huge bite each, then they start back down the same way they came. I watch them come and go, come and go, one after another.

They are really very orderly creatures, ants; they remind me of tiny soldiers. They're all walking in a single file, swaying their out-of-proportioned heads from side to side, resembling a band of thirsty dogs. One after another they clamp down on the sandwich and walk back carrying crumb after crumb. I'm nearly hypnotized by them, with the sun blocking out all the other objects around me. Crumb after crumb disappears before my eyes until the entire sandwich is completely gone, and not until the last ant disappears over the ledge do I sit up.

They will take over the world one day, I say, and Charlie reaches her hand out and removes a black hair of hers that is caught on my lip.

I'm still feeling a bit dizzy so we take a cab and ride it all the way down to Union Square. Charlie is sitting close to me, her head leaning on my shoulder, and I let her. I let her because she seems very comfortable and relaxed, but mostly because I don't have the energy to stir things up. She keeps her eyes closed all the way and relaxes in a great big yawn, and out of the blue I suggest we go see a movie.

We get out on the busy corner of Broadway and Union Square. There are thousands of people around and smoke from a hot dog vendor by the curb is blowing our way. Music is pumping from a store and the smoke stings my eyes so I can't see a thing. I walk with my hand on Charlie's shoulder and seconds later we step inside some place and leave the street behind. As we walk I feel her bones moving under my hand, under her skin.

On the inside it's cool and I take a seat for a second as Charlie goes to the bathroom. For once it's not me. I close my eyes and feel her watching me, from somewhere, but even as she leaves I don't want to get up. I tell myself it's because I'm tired, that my eyes hurt, and it will be over soon anyway. I lean forward and rest my face in my palms. The door next to me opens every now and then; I can feel the wind on my legs and smell the smoke. Someone passes me so close that their coat brushes against my head, and as I open my eyes, I see my son.

Charlie comes back from the bathroom and she's smiling. I can tell she's happy that I'm still here. Or perhaps she's just happy, it really is hard to tell with girls.

Let's see this one, I say and point to the

poster that sits on the wall right across from us.

The 39 Steps. It's a remake of the classic Hitchcock and I think it came out sometime in the 30s, but I'm not sure.

We ride the escalator to the third floor and now it's my turn to go. When I come back Charlie is holding a giant bucket of popcorn and I surprise myself. Right at this moment, if I could choose, I don't want her to disappear at all. At this very moment I actually want to see this movie with her.

We are a bit late so we take the two seats nearest the entrance. It's not even half-full and we put our coats on the seats next to us. I don't tell her about my son, or that I've seen the movie before for that matter. I don't tell her I've seen it many times before because it used to be Phoebe's favorite.

It's just after the show at London Music Hall where Mr. Memory demonstrates his supernatural power of recall. Suddenly shots are fired. I look over at Charlie and she's already into the movie, breathing through her open mouth. The main characters find each other in a rumble after a panic breaks out. The two of them then go back to his apartment where she tells him she is really a spy. The colors seemed brighter in the old version, although everything is much clearer now. Shadows dance over Charlie's and my own face, my son's shadow. Was it the cottage where we spent the early summers that Phoebe told my son about the movie? I know everything that is about to happen before it actually does.

Watch out, I say just before the scene where the girl is stabbed with a bread knife and the guy sneaks out of the apartment disguised as a milkman and takes a train to Scotland.

Shhhh! Charlie hushes at me but I can see that she's not upset.

Heads up, I say as the man with the missing finger-joint shoots him.

Charlie pushes my face away and focuses on the screen. When they are once again at the show of Mr. Memory and the movie is about to end, Charlie doesn't even bother to take her hand away. She keeps it slung across my arm, the back of her hand resting against my chest.

Throughout the entire movie I try not to think of him. I'm very proud but I try not to think. Then it's finally the part where the guy yells, *What are the 39 steps?* Phoebe used to lip-sync that.

Then Mr. Memory starts rambling, *The 39 steps is an organization of spies, collecting information on behalf of the foreign office of...* and then someone shoots him.

Even though I knew how it would end, deep inside I was still hoping for something else. Deep inside I was hoping for something about the past to have changed.

As we walk through the door it's just getting dark. I notice the streets are wet from rain. Puddles of water glisten off the neon reflecting from the sign on the wall above us. It's become a dreamy place with all that light jumping from puddle to puddle, following alongside us as we walk. It is in fact a dream, I remember. I have started dreaming again. The hand I'm holding wouldn't be there otherwise. My face feels flushed but the hand in mine is even hotter. I might as well be carrying a piece of glowing hot coal. We keep it like that in the taxi. We look out the window, each on our own side, and we don't say a thing. We let go well before we reach the lobby.

The night is the same as before. Charlie is in her chair wrapped in a blanket and I'm on my back in the bed. For a short while my heart is racing and I'm wide awake.

16

When I wake up the chair is empty. There's a note on the floor beside my bed that's written on the backside of a page torn from a book. At the end of the note she writes, **Meet me there at nine.**

I flip the paper over and I see that it's the last page of a book. I mean, I can't say for sure what book it is, as I don't recognize the text, but it has something final about it. That's how I'm sure it's the end of something.

Apart from going down for breakfast I spend the entire day inside. I skip lunch and walk around my room, starting from the desk and over to the window, and then back. A day is both long and short this way. Standing in the middle of it, it's as if it will never end, but when the sun begins to bleed over the west, I'm not sure it has even taken place. I watch it, how it is lowering down and how blood fills the surface before it begins to boil. Then, when the last of the roundness is buried, I walk over to the desk and sit down. For a long time I hold the pen one inch from the paper and I think of the right things to say. One hundred times I start in my head, but none of it makes it onto the paper. It shouldn't be this hard. My own flesh and blood. I close my eyes for a second and look back. *Dear.... My Dear.... I know it's been long... I think about you often... I love you...* I drop the pen and push the notepad to the side.

It's still much too early, I have lots of time left, but I get up and take my hat and leave anyway. I get off at 24th Street and walk all the way down to the corner of St. Marks and Astor Place. There a man is sitting on the ground with his back against the fence. In front of him is a spread out blanket with piles of books and some old records, and next to him stands a row of paintings. I suppose the guy is homeless because he looks sort of down and out, but that kills me even more. A homeless man with books and paintings.

He is working on something and I lean over

to the side and catch a glimpse of the sketchpad he's balancing on his lap. Even though it's upside down I can see it's a flower. In fact, when I look around at the other paintings, I can see that all of them are, although this particular one has a center like a shining sun. The man looks up from his pad, smiles at me and nods a silent hello. I nod back and we are just two old fellows greeting each other. It's a silent recognition of age, the way the thought of death ties one man to another.

I'm already in the right place so I have nothing to do but to wait. I take a step closer and look at the things he has displayed on the ground. The records aren't new at all. They are big old 45s, with titles like *Jesus Christ Superstar, Dancing Queen* and other classics, and the books, the books are really about everything from history to gardening, and then, of course, there are the paintings.

The one to the far left catches my eye right away. It's not a complicated piece but there's something about it that speaks to me. It's of another sunflower, but in black and white, and it has unnaturally long vines that climb around the entire paper like a Jack and the Beanstalk plant. It's painted on some kind of cardboard and framed with what looks to be different colors of driftwood.

Twenty-five dollars, he says before I even get a chance to ask about the price.

His voice is warm and smooth, not a voice you'd expect to find on the street at all. I look around to see if she's arrived and then I dig out 30 dollars and hand it to him. He gives me five back, but I only shake my head and smile.

I don't even have a wall to hang it on, I say, but it's mostly to myself.

I carry my painting over to the side and ease myself down next to him with my back against the fence.

How are things? he asks, and I turn to look at him.

His dark, sweet voice is not very loud, it's more than a whisper really, but it's the sort of whisper that carries. Most people are shadows until you turn to look at them and it's not until you do that you really see them. The way his tired eyes look at me, the way they're sort of on a slant, is the same way Frock used to look at me. Good old Frock.

I'm George, the man says and his hand feels very warm in mine.

George is sitting on a pile of used books and he still keeps the worn sketchbook in his lap. After its brief contact with mine, his hand glides backwards the same way it came. It snakes through the air and disappears into his pocket. I lean back and look out over the dark street. There's a good sort of silence between us. The kind you feel you needn't untangle.

You ever had a dog, George? I say.

The question makes him look up from his

pad and at first it's as if he doesn't understand.

Dog?

Yeah, I say. You ever had a dog?

His hand starts moving across the sketchpad, tracing and retracing line after line until he has breathed life into it and the flower is on fire.

I'm from down in Louisiana, he says. There were dogs all around there.

A burly looking guy with long hair and tattoo-covered arms stops in front of us. He puts his hand out and meets George's clenched fist in midair. They both grunt something but I can't hear what, and when he leaves, two cigarettes and some coins magically appears in George's hand.

I shake my head when he offers me one and press on.

What I mean is, did you ever have a dog of your own?

George places a cigarette between his lips, looks through his pocket and pulls out a lighter.

No, I suppose I never did have a dog of my own, he says, and he lights the cigarette.

Moments later, through a smoke filled exhale, he adds,

If it's even possible to own one.

I look at the sleeping stone giant, the building across the street, while George continues to add line after line to his flower.

I have two of them in there, George says without looking up.

Cooper Union, he continues, built in 1910 and home to the first ever spherical elevator.

The world is very still for a moment and for a second it kills me. Still today, on the last stretch of life, it manages to kill me. I guess some things you just never realize until you sit on a street corner.

I look around, at every stopping cab, at every passing person on the sidewalk across the street, I try to see Charlie, but there's no sight of her. I wait until George is done with the last line and his hand is completely still before I say it.

I'm not who you think I am.

Comments like this are really meant to be reserved for a heart-to-heart between two old friends, but I've never been very good at opening up to other people. And if I ever do, I find it easier to say such things to strangers. George doesn't say anything, or even look up. He seems to be thinking it over. For a few seconds there is complete silence between us, then George pours his sweet voice over it, but it's not the answer I had expected.

A poem I once read goes like this. 'Live and let live, dig and be dug in return.'

Then there's a few seconds pause, before he punctuates it.

Yeah, he says, that's what I live by.

I'm not really sure he understood what I just said, I want to tell him everything that has happened to me lately. I feel this urge to share it with someone but the only thing I do is repeat it slowly in my mind. Live and let live, dig and be dug in return.

Two middle-aged men step out from a door of Cooper Union and walk over to where we are sitting. One of them carries a book under his arm and he hands it to George.

I read it. Thank you, he says, and George nods his head and puts the book on the ground next to the others for sale.

The two men walk away towards the subway station and then George answers my question without even hearing it.

I guess it means that when you love something you get love in return, George says.

I let that sink in, and I look at him from an angle. I mean, I really look at him good, and what I see isn't a fellow sitting on the sidewalk because he has nothing else to do; what I see is a fellow sitting on the sidewalk because there is nothing else he wants to do.

My knees hurt like hell when I stand up.

I should be on my way, I say, even though there's no sight of Charlie yet.

I pick up my painting, tuck it under my arm and put my hand down to George. The warmth from him spreads into my fingers and travels up my arm and all the way into my chest.

I've only taken a few steps before he calls for me.

Say, man!

I stop and turn around.

What you got that makes you jump?

George is standing up now and I feel his eyes on me.

We all need that, you know. Something that makes us jump.

He looks at me the same way a cat peers out at the strangeness of people from a dark alley and I can tell he knows I don't haven an answer, but still he wants to see me off with the question.

See ya around, George, I say and wave goodbye again.

He's wrong though, about me not having an answer. I do have an answer but it's not an answer he would expect. Come to think of it, it's not an answer at all, it's another question. And the question I don't give him is: What have I really got that makes me not want to jump?

I see Charlie standing by the light just down the street from George. She spots the painting under my arm and even before she says anything, I know what it will be.

I like the flower, Mr. C.

I don't know if the fact that I'm showing up means anything, if it's some sort of promise, but I try not to think of it. The light changes from red to green, to red, and then to green again. Charlie is wearing a flowery dress and worn cowboy boots out of which her legs stand straight as fern trees, firmly planted on the sidewalk. A glittery scarf is wrapped around her neck but it still looks cold.

I wasn't sure you would come, she says.

I am an old man standing on a street corner with a flower painting stuck under my arm. Next to me is my old student who has a crush on her old teacher. This is just a detour, I tell myself, and I take her arm and we walk across the street at the next green light.

You hungry? I ask her.

We walk up St.Marks Place and it sure has changed a lot. It used to be a residential street but has now turned into a miniature Tivoli for kids with tattoos and bones sticking out of their noses. We find a Japanese restaurant on the first floor where the tables are really small and cut out of a single piece of wood. I lean the painting against the wall next to the table and we sit down across from each other.

Charlie has a frail face, much like her body, but you can tell there's strength on the inside. If I could choose one feature that makes her stand out, that contains her beauty, I would say it is her lips most of all, although they are very hard to describe. I ask the waitress for the bathroom and she points me through a corridor. When I come back there's a bottle of sake on the table.

I ordered some appetizers while you were gone, she says.

She talks about her school, she's still in

school, and suddenly I feel very old.

I guess you can't really *study* art, she says.

She shows me some of her paintings on her cell phone. There's one there that interests me more than the others. It's a collage of a woman eating ice cream while baring her breasts. The breasts and the ice cream aren't two separate things; the ice cream is in a giant cone that is part of the woman's body and her breasts are part of the scoops of ice cream. Even though I look hard I can't see where it begins and where it ends and I think that's why I like it.

Charlie keeps talking about art and paintings and her school. The words flow from her mouth and in the middle of a sentence it's clear to me what George meant.

Art makes you jump, I say.

It's not really put as a question but Charlie stops in the middle of a sentence and at once she becomes serious and still on the other side of the table. Just then, when the silence has spread like a carpet of prickly nails between us, our waitress comes in carrying plates of food. There are dumplings, a soup with two empty bowls, sautéed mushrooms and fish on a stick.

Don't talk like that, she says quietly and looks at me coolly between the waitress's arms.

I look away and turn my attention to the fish. They are very small fish, with a skewer going through them from head to tail and I can't help but feel a bit sorry for the poor bastards. I just can't. I feel more comfortable looking at the fish than I do at Charlie right now, so I pick one up and hold it in front of my face. It's so silvery perfect.

Have you heard of Stockhausen? I ask and turn the fish to face her way. I hide behind it and bounce it up and down as I speak with my most intellectual Cambridge voice.

He wrote the Helikopterstreich-quartett, among others, I continue.

I can hear Charlie smile and shake her head, even though I don't really see her behind the fish.

It was a piece created by Karl Heinz Stockhausen in 1993, in which each member of a string quartet presided over a helicopter transformed into a flying studio, combining the instrumental sounds with the whirring of the propeller.

As I finish I turn the stick around, and headfirst, I pull the entire fish off with my teeth.

She's not upset anymore.

You know, sometimes you are just too much, Mr. C, she says and picks up the bottle of sake.

She fills the miniature cups to the brim with the milky white substance and holds hers up, waiting for me.

Cheers, she says, and I throw my head back and let the liquid warm my throat before it collects in a small pool at the bottom of my stomach.

The sake does something to me and my hands come to life and pick up the painting from the floor and start turning it around. Waiters rush by carrying steaming hot dishes and before I know it our table is filled with an array of plates and the cup is full again.

Every Wednesday he wore a yellow shirt or sweater, I say, because it symbolizes openness, love, collaboration and universality.

We eat and Charlie seems to stuff all her food in her cheeks. Two round balls have formed there but still she keeps picking up more bits of mushroom and cauliflower with her chopsticks and pushing them in between her lips. We drink yet another cup of sake and the pool grows.

I love yellow, she says, and we drink another cup and then another, and what was once a pool has now become an ocean.

We are the last to leave and as we walk back towards Astor Place the bottoms of my feet have become rounded, making me roll, first forward, every step I take, and then backward. George is gone and I don't bother telling Charlie about him. All the records, books and paintings are gone too; there's no trace of him, save for a few cigarette butts on the ground. We stop on the corner to wait for the light to change and on the top of the garbage pail I see the books. I recognize some of them and Charlie picks out three that she wants to keep.

The streets are empty and we don't have anywhere we are heading so we just walk. The cool air feels good on my warm head. Everything in my body is warm, my hands, my head, even the tip of my nose that is usually always cold.

I'll walk you home, I say, and she hands me the books to carry. It's as if I'm back in high school.

We walk down Broadway and I'm holding the painting under one arm and a pack of books under the other. I feel the ocean inside me move with every step I take.

About halfway to Houston St. we come upon a huge light suspended high above the street. It shines in the direction we are going, lighting up a piece of the sidewalk. It's been sprayed with water and it glimmers mysteriously in the light. At the end of the wet part stands a group of people, and beyond them are cameras mounted on high chairs. Except for the ones standing in front of the cameras, we are the only other people out, and we enter the wet area from the top and walk towards the group. I'm sure we're a sight to see. A young woman in cowboy boots and a flowery dress, walking next to an old man with a pack of books under one arm and a flower painting tucked under the other.

Smile, I whisper to her, you're a movie star.

The group of people part without a word as we get to the end and we turn the corner and follow a cobblestone street over to Lafayette. We turn again and walk south and on Spring Street we pass a small creature that doesn't look like anything I've ever seen before; a ghost mixed with an astronaut.

He's only about a foot high and he has been drawn on the asphalt right next to the crosswalk.

He's fabulous! Charlie exclaims, and she begins taking pictures of it with her phone.

She wants me to pose with it and I crouch down as far as I can, but still my face is too far from the ground. All the pictures ever show is part of my legs next to that strange creature.

We keep going and walk down Bowery and not long after that we come across a table standing on the sidewalk. It's a nice old table and it's just standing there the way you'd think someone had just brought it out only minutes ago. We sit down on it and discover it's precisely the right height. All in all, it's a nice little table, and it's a nice little night.

My bladder is complaining and I get up and go across the street to find a sheltered place. It's strange because I've hardly seen any other people, but as I take a leak against a graffiti covered door around the corner, I hear music coming from inside. At least I know that the world is still here.

Back at the table Charlie is doing some stretches. She's becoming more and more like a cat every time I look at her and it gives me an idea.

Walk with this on your head, I say and hand her a book.

I place one on my own head and walk behind her very slowly. Good old Pencey. Seems like a million years ago.

We both drop the books about five times each before we've had enough. The books are all beat up but Charlie still wants to keep them, so I take them in my hand and we keep going until we come to an open diner. It's sort of on a side street and a strange place to have a diner in the first place, but Charlie wants a root beer float so we step inside. But the man behind the counter says they don't serve root beer floats at this hour so we continue down Bowery without talking.

It's now closer to morning than it is to night and the sky is slowly fading from deep darkness to a lighter blue. I listen to the sounds our shoes make against the sidewalk; it's a rhythmic tapping, and I feel the ocean inside me has all but disappeared and what's left is only a dried up desert surrounding a patch of wetness.

You know what the measure of a good evening is? I turn and ask her.

Tell me, she says, and then shakes her head with a tired motion.

We are on the street outside her building and it's very dirty; old salad leaves and pieces of cardboard cover the ground. I try to see the birds through the window but it's too dark.

It's coming home with things you didn't leave with, I say as I hand her the books.

I'm about to hand her the painting as well when she suddenly steps past me into the street. I hear a taxi stop with a shriek behind my back, and she gets in and leaves the door towards the sidewalk open. I stand there for a while, not sure if I kissed her cheek goodbye or not, then I get into the cab and we ride together uptown.

The room is flooded in steel blue morning light and stepping inside feels just like stepping into a swimming pool. Charlie moves over to the window while I stand in one spot inside the door. I sit down on the bed and take my shoes off, and they make a tumbling, hollow sound as I drop them on the floor. It's possible the sound woke up the guest in the room below, and if it was possible to see through the floor, that very same guest would have seen how I got up and walked straight over to the window, put my hand on Charlie's shoulder, and spun her around.

Oh my God, if it was possible to see through thoughts. She presses her lips against mine, harder than I press against hers, and I feel her hands clasp at the back of my suit. Both of us are blue. We have blue hair and blue skin and when I release my grip so does Charlie. My lips are moist and taste sweet like I can't remember they've tasted ever before.

It's late, I say and hurry over to the bathroom and lock myself in.

I shower for a long time and leave my clothes in a pile on the floor. When I come out I see her on the bed. She's on her side with her back to me, sleeping like a child. Carefully I lay down on my back and immediately, the same moment she feels the tension of the surface change, the fly dangling in the spiders web, she rolls from the wall and slings one arm across my chest. Her leg follows her arm and in one smooth motion she slides on top of me.

She locks her lips to mine. Her skin is warm and soft and her breath moves from her nose and mouth into my body, where it drops something off, and then returns the same way it came. She sucks on my lower lip but I keep my tongue still and I close my eyes and drift away.

Inside I'm light as a feather and I float softly downwards, down, down and down. When I land I'm back at the bottom of the river, only this time Molly isn't here; I'm all alone. Something is moving behind me but I can't make out much of anything because of the murky water. The only thing I really see is myself and when I look down I notice I'm completely naked, and that I have an erection. All of a sudden something comes at me from behind. It's some sort of animal, octopus-like with long arms, but I don't see it; I only feel it. I feel it first on my shoulder but I'm afraid to turn around and get it in my face, so I just sit very still. But it has found me now and it wanders forward; it seems to have one hundred little legs. It doesn't matter that I sit still; it moves over me until it covers my ear and I hear it whisper.

I love the smell of old things.

The creature has a female voice. I see now that the

black animal is back and it's pressing itself down over my face; only this time it's trying to push into my mouth.

I shake my head from side to side and roll my body to get free. I roll harder and faster and I feel my erection roll with me, but still the animal is there, pushing into my mouth. With the last of my breath I grab what I can and pull on it with all my strength. The animal bites down hard on my lip and I hear Charlie let out a loud scream.

I taste blood in my mouth and in my hand there's something soft. When I open my eyes I see Charlie propped against the wall, her chest heaving violently. She rubs the back of her head and looks at me with a wild stare.

I...I can't, I say and let go of my grip. Not with you, I add, but I regret it the moment I say it.

Charlie jumps out of bed and only seconds later she is dressed. I notice we are both still blue.

I'm not sure I hear what I think I hear, or if it's just the door.

Crazy bastard it sounds like, but I think it's just the door. As soon as she's gone I lay on my back and when I sleep I don't dream, not even about the tapping.

When I wake up my lip hurts and there's some dried blood on my pillow. I'm standing in the shower when I hear the door open and close and I hurry out with only a towel around my waist.

I'm sorry, I begin but I cut myself short when I see the boy.

He's sitting in the chair by the window and Charlie is curled up in his lap. I can see that she's different just from taking one look at her. The boy gets up and comes over to me while Charlie goes and stands by the window, and for a moment I have this crazy thought that he's going to take a swing at me. But all he does is extend his hand.

Thanks man, he says. This is something we've been wanting to do.

I feel naked even though I'm wearing the towel and I really want to get dressed, but the boy has walked around me and I'd have to go around *him* in order to get to the bathroom, so I just stand there.

Why don't you sit over here? the boy says and points to the chair.

Charlie hasn't even looked me in the eyes. She walks over to the boy and gets up on her toes and whispers something in his ear.

The boy smiles a devilish grin, and says,

So, gramps, you like to watch little girls?

I can see that Charlie is blushing but still she doesn't look at me.

I can't help but stare when they kiss. It's the longest kiss I've ever seen. Both their tongues come out and they aren't even tongues, it's a pair of snakes tangled up in a wrestling match. They slurp and suck on each other as if the world has disappeared and I feel chilly all over. Charlie keeps both her hands in his back pockets as they walk over to the bed. This floor must have seen thousands of footsteps through-out time, but I bet nothing ever like this before.

In a matter of seconds they are completely naked. Charlie is on her back and her nipples are in his mouth. Even though I have goosebumps on my arms, my face is burning red-hot. Nobody is blue anymore. The light is cold and hard and through it I listen to her moan and squirm as the boy moves further down. The mattress doesn't squeak or make any sound at all, it's a good mattress that way. Not even when the boy starts to move faster and faster does it make any sound. Charlie moans, careful at first, then louder and louder, one step higher and higher, and eventually it is as if she's crying. Then, suddenly, they stop and everything becomes quiet. She gets on top of him and for the first time since this morning she looks me in the eyes.

Her hair is thicker than I remember, even if it was just hours ago. It's now a little hat that goes all around her head, and she looks at me through eyes drawn into thin slits. She moves slowly at first, up and down, forward and backward, around in a circular motion, then faster and faster. All the while never letting go of my eyes. I think it's drops of sweat that fall from her cheek and make her breasts shine, but I'm not sure.

The mattress keeps quiet but inside my

head a terrible sound has now begun. It began as a distant tapping but quickly turned into a mighty ruckus. It's not just the tapping sound this time, it's also a pouring noise. Like that of a wild mountain stream cutting right through my head. Charlie is moving faster and faster and it's as if the noise in my head increases for every moan she makes and every breath she takes. The tapping and the stream try to break each other and they both get louder and louder and I can no longer focus on the bed. Tears fill my eyes and everything is spinning and the pressure inside me has built up so enormously that I am afraid my pipes will burst any second. There's nothing for me to do but to open my head up and let it out. That's really the only thing I can think of and I put my hands on top of my head from the sides and I try to bend my skull apart to get the sound out. I try to dig my fingers through my scalp to get a grip on the bone, but I can't get through. Then everything stops, just like that. As fast as it came the sound has gone away, in a flash of a moment, and I feel fine again. There's no pain, no more sound, and all I do is wipe my tears away and then I feel just like normal again.

It's when I open my eyes that I get the next surprise. Both of them are gone. I don't mean they're gone in the way that they have left; I mean they're completely gone. The bed looks like it has been done by the maid, with perfectly folded creases and identical lengths on each side, and their clothes are gone from the floor, and so are they. There's not one single trace of them ever being here. I get up and look under the bed but they are not there either. I look in the closet without finding anything but empty hangars. I look in the bathroom but only find my pile of dirty clothes. I even open the door and look up and down the hallway, but still, nothing. The two of them have gone up in smoke.

Perhaps it's finally setting in, what's been swimming peacefully in my blood for so long. I have always feared I would end like this but I figured it would be more subtle at first. I imagined it would start with forgetting peoples names, then their birthdays, and later even the ability to keep track of the days of the week. But this seems to be it. I'm finally turning into Phoebe.

Ha ha! So the world is in order once again! With a little push of my thumb she's flicked off the page like a piece of dirt. The longer we go the more I'm learning there are ways around the holes. Yes, there are holes I never knew of, bottomless pits like wormholes where some of them fall in and continue up on the other side, then sprout in a new spot like a mushroom.

But I'm on him. I can taste his blood and I see he's tiring. I'm on him now and won't let go.

17

I take my time walking down there. I make a left at the hotel and I walk east in the direction of the river. It takes me 35 minutes to reach the East Side Park and I walk right across the ball field and continue over the gravel path, all the way out to the rocks by the water. I pick a smooth round stone and sit down.

The river flows north today. Some days it flows north and some south, but mostly it flows south. For a thousand years that's how the river has been flowing. Up and down.

You are not my friend, I say to the water.

I don't say it very loud, I just say it to say it. The river doesn't make a sound, even though hundreds of tons of water are flowing by every second. I stand up and say it again, but this time I shout it.

You are not my friend!

I hear the 'my friend' part echo once before dying down in the distance. It loosens something in my chest, the screaming, so I continue.

Nothing but grief!

I listen to the echo and try to hear it as many times as I can, but I only really hear the 'f' this time.

I am an animal!

I face the river and I scream from the top of my lungs.

Two hundred years ago!

Spit comes flying out of my mouth for every word that leaves it.

Set the clocks! Tallyho! I just scream what pops into my mind.

AAAAAAHHHHHHHHHHHHH!

My chest is heaving up and down and I'm breathing hard. I stand there and I look out over the water, at how my drowning echoes are helplessly taken out to sea and it doesn't matter. Nothing of this matters where I'm going. I can't believe I let myself get side tracked like that and let precious time go to waste. Nothing of this matters because only Mary matters. I bend down and scoop up a handful of water and I drink it.

My head is empty of ideas and the only place I can think to look is the library. I know this is not the way to do it, that you can't just step up to the counter and ask for a guide on how to kill yourself, but right now I don't have any other ideas.

I get into a cab and my driver is a big fellow with an enormous head. He keeps it tilted to one side just so it will fit under the roof, and as soon as I get in he starts talking.

You have all these people gone over the weekend, he says, but it seems to be directed more to the cab in general, like he's already halfway through telling a story that started with his first passenger this morning and will end with the last. I pretend I haven't heard him.

Ya said the library, right?

I see myself nod in the rearview mirror.

Gotcha, just checkin.

Christ, he's only had one minute to forget.

By tonight everything is going to be packed, bumper to bumper. People coming back from the weekend, he says.

We keep moving and the big head continues to talk all the way.

I used to live in Europe, in Amsterdam. I used to live everywhere. But I remember Amsterdam because of the vacation.

I let his voice fill the background while I look at the buildings, the lamp posts and the street corners that pass outside the window. It used to be that things were new. At least for a little while. Now everywhere I go it seems I have been there before.

We pull up outside the library and the driver doesn't stop talking, even though I'm on my way out of the car.

Amsterdam. Whisky and hashish, I'll tell you. Amsterdam and Montreal are the hashish capitals of the world.

I close the door and start walking up the stone steps.

But it takes your desire away!

I see him lean across the front seat and scream the last part through the crack in the rolled down window.

I bet that if I draw a straight line, a line that cuts through time, through every taxi ride I have ever taken, they would all somehow end up here. I mean, some things are meant to be, no matter how many taxi rides there are in between. Some things are just fixed that way. The same way I get out of the cab and walk up all those stone steps, while picturing Giant Head deep in the corner of a smoke-filled bar, his eyes bright red from the smoke and his head towering above it all like a cloud covered mountaintop, and when I reach the last step I somehow know the answer.

Drugs are the answer. I turn on my heel and walk down the steps and I cross the street to the pharmacy. Inside it's very silent and all the aisles are empty. I float down each one under the fluorescent light, passing vitamins and minerals, allergy relief, eye drops and lotions, and there's something hypnotizing about it. I feel like I could float in front of colorful bottles forever. But then I find it.

The bottle says 1 pill every three hours, not more than 4 times a day, and I take the one containing 100 pills and pay at the counter. I'm amazed at how decisive I am, how I seem to know exactly what to do, when not long ago I was completely lost.

As I walk towards the exit my ears picks up on a sound that I recognize from somewhere. It's something from deep down inside, a sudden thump that's been there before, and when I get outside and look around the sidewalk, my memory my memory catches up with me. How fantastic. I see it laying on the ground next to the wall. There's a drop of blood between it's beaks and on the glass above my head is a fatty smudge stain.

How extraordinarily fantastic, I whisper, and I tighten the grip on my plastic bag and bend down to get a better look.

I'm not sure why but I decide to go back to the park again and I take another cab to get there. It doesn't really matter where I go as long as there aren't too many people around, there's just something about the park that pulls me in.

This driver has a normal sized head and his name is Frank. Frank looks an awful lot like he's from India but I suppose it doesn't matter one way or the other where he is from, or how he got his name, as long as he gets us where we're going.

I get off at the Museum of Natural History and walk north, deep into the heart of the park. As soon as I have passed the reservoir there will be fewer people around. I walk forward under the trees and every time a leaf falls and settles to the ground something inside me stirs.

Even from a distance I know it's the one. Placed under a giant oak tree, it faces west. The bench has sort of chosen itself and I can think of nothing more appropriate than the afternoon sun on my face when I go. The sun is high in the sky, it's still a bit too early, and I sit back and just watch the park. I feel my bladder as a pinching sensation at the base of my spine and as I stand behind the oak tree with one hand resting on it's rough surface, I find it strange to think of the last thing one does. Like the last time you take a piss behind a tree.

I remember the trees from when I was a kid. We've grown old together and now I will leave them. It doesn't feel like anything in particular; it's just the way it is. Things are much clearer now, things around me, I mean. They come out of the canvas and I can reach out and run my fingers over every detail and every thought. I listen to my heart, to how it ticks. I think of my son, I think of my parents, I think of Allie, D.B., and Phoebe. I give them each five minutes and I make up a collage of the best parts. All the memories are many years old and, even though I try hard to see them, they are still muddled. The one movie I don't replay is the one with Mary. I'll see her in just a bit.

Every now and then someone walks by, a jogger or someone with a dog on a leash, but I don't look up. I see their feet enter the strip of gravel from one side, and I see them leave on the other. The sun is on its downwards arc now but it's still a bit too early. I feel my bladder again but this time I ignore it and for the first time since the pharmacy I open my hand and let go of the bag.

I have to use my teeth to get the plastic seal off the bottle. The pills look so small in my hand and perhaps it's because of the light, but they seem to have a yellowish color. I don't bother counting them, there looks to be more than twenty in my palm. Drops of sweat trickle down my back and collect at the hem of my pants, but my hand is still steady. I don't know what the last thought should be, what makes most sense. I simply try to see them all together in a room, then I kiss my open hand goodbye.

I hold the pills on my tongue while I open the bottle of water. The bitterness spreads quickly throughout my mouth and a slight panic rises in my chest as the tapping begins. It's coming from the area right above my left ear, about an inch inside my head, and it's hard and fast, like a drum roll it sounds very determined. Slowly the image of the room fades away and I pinch my leg and try with all my might to get back in. I concentrate on the bitter taste and I try to ignore the tapping. It's just a sound, I tell myself, just a sound, and after a minute I've made it back. I close my eyes and breathe there.

When I open my eyes again I look into the eyes of another. A young boy is staring straight at me and a woman who must be his mother is pulling on his arm, trying to get him to move. But the boy refuses to budge and keeps staring straight at me. He's got big round eyes and, like a butterfly pinned to the wall, I see my own reflection in them.

Come on, John.

The woman speaks with some sort of accent and I get the impression that perhaps she isn't his mother at all, but a nanny.

John still refuses to move, but his eyes do. I follow them across my shoulder to my arm, down to the open can of pills on the bench.

Come on, John, let's go!

We lock eyes again, the way two cowboys at sundown would. We have nothing to shoot with, yet I feel bullets pierce my skin and enter my heart. There's no doubt about it, it's in his eyes. I am the bad guy that will be left in the dust where the horse drawn carriages won't even try to avoid running me over. The woman pulls on John's arm again, this time more violently, and he starts to stumble forward. The light is honey golden on our skin. Finally, as the sun is just right, they move away from me. But John's eyes never leave mine, not until they disappear around the bend.

Beads of sweat have gathered on my forehead and I shove two fingers down my throat and turn to the side. The pills have melted into a mush but even on the way up they taste bitter.

Not with kids around, I whisper to myself.

I sit on the bench for a long time without moving. I get up once to go behind the oak tree to empty my bladder again, and then I just sit. The bottle is somewhere behind me, the pills scattered across the grass, and my heart is beating fast, as if I have been running very long and hard. I think of Stradlater, from out of nowhere, and what he said about the gloves, and then I get up.

I do it too quickly and I have to grab hold of the back of the bench until the dizziness clears. Then I start walking and I don't stop until I'm way over on the other side of the park.

I've made up my mind, but I have to rest for a minute before I go in. I sit at the top of the stairs and take off my hat; I hold it in my hand and I watch the kids on the playground across the street. I can't really see what they are doing, being so far away and all that they've become tiny ants. I suppose they're running and jumping, the normal kids stuff, but it would still have been nice to see them better.

A hotdog man pushes his cart forward on the sidewalk below. It's heavy and he has to dig his heels in to keep it moving. When he stops by the dark green streetlight he begins opening and closing all sorts of hatches on the back. I watch him all around me groups of kids pass me where I sit. When you're in school you always come here a lot. They scream and laugh and pull on each other's backpacks, and it kills me how their sneakers look way too big for their feet.

I put my hat back on just to feel how well it fits. I like that feeling, how nothing seems to be between me and the hat. I take it off and put it back on and it sinks into place perfectly. I take it off and put it on again, and I keep doing it, and every time it settles on my head perfectly. The hotdog man has finished his setup and is serving his first customers, an old woman and a little girl. The old woman takes the hotdog and hands it to the little girl who has to let go of her coat in order to take it. She looks so tiny next to the woman and the hotdog stand. Suddenly I drop the hat and it tumbles down the stairs and I have to get up to retrieve it. I still feel dizzy but on my way back up the stairs I continue directly inside.

The girl at the counter informs me that there's only one spot left.

You're lucky, she says, but I don't really know what she's talking about.

I just step over to where she is pointing, towards a small group of people standing across the room, and I walk to the back without speaking to anyone. By the way, it's not true what they say, that time stands still in a museum, because when I let my head drop backwards I see a map of the world painted on the ceiling and I don't remember ever seeing it there before.

Suddenly the line starts moving and I follow along across the hall and then through a door in the side wall. We're not that many, perhaps ten of us and I hear someone speak Japanese. Without warning the line stops abruptly and each person bumps into the one ahead.

There will be no speaking unless you have specific questions about the tour.

It's a tiny little voice coming from the front, and then, just as sudden, the line starts moving again.

We continue down a stairwell and go through a long underground hallway that echoes with our footsteps, before we stop outside a thick steel door covered in many round instruments. A tiny man, the man with the tiny voice, stands in front of the door and tells us that the freezers are where they keep the animals when they reorganize the exhibits.

He himself looks like some sort of animal when he speaks, moving his brawny arms and short legs from side to side.

I forbid you to touch anything as we step

inside, he says and looks at us sternly before turning a huge lever, and the door swings open.

A whoosh escapes from the door and everybody takes one step back as a cloud of icy white fog rises to the ceiling. The man holds the door open and lets us in, one by one, and this time the Japanese couple ends up right in front of me. They smile and bob their heads up and down as they turn to face me, then the woman returns to staring at everything around us with great round eyes. The tiny man closes the door behind and walks past us all, up to the front again. I can't really hear anything from where I'm standing in the back but it doesn't matter.

The freezer consists of many rooms, all connected by a door less entry on each end, and I can't help but look at all the things as we pass through the rooms. The way we pass animals standing on pallets along the walls; open crates with hairy backs sticking up; shelves crammed with multicolored birds of all shapes and sizes, makes it feel just like walking through a frozen jungle.

Suddenly the idea is just there. I hadn't known exactly how before the line stops, but as it does suddenly I do. It stops only for a minute and as it begins to move again I stay where I am. I don't say a word, I just stand still and watch the end of the line move away from me. The moment before it disappears completely around the bend the Japanese woman turns around and sees me standing there. She's got this frightened look on her face that seems to say, *No, please don't upset the tiny man*, but she doesn't open her mouth. I form my own mouth around a couple of words but white smoke is all that comes out. Three times is a charm.

When I'm sure they're gone I start walking back the way we came from to try and find a good spot. I'm halfway when I feel my bladder cramp up. It's probably because of the pills and all and it hurts so much I have to lean forward until the muscles in my stomach have relaxed. It only lasts a few seconds.

As I stand up I release the big furry hand I grabbed when I bent down – or I should really say paw. The huge stuffed bear is standing on its back legs on a wooden platform. It's almost twice as tall as I am and has a massive body. His paws are stretched out, clawing at some invisible prey, and his white teeth glow like ice picks about to drop above my head. I go over to the corner and relieve myself behind a crate with an anteater, then I walk back to the bear. It truly is a magnificent creature, a beast from the past. It once roamed wild somewhere in Alaska or Canada, piercing ten-pound salmons on its claws before throwing them up on the riverbank with a flick of his wrist. And this is where he ended up. Life sure is mysterious.

The platform is big enough for me to lay down on and I rest my head on one of the furry bear feet. I don't feel cold at all. I'm wearing my hat but no gloves, but I still don't feel cold. I listen to the humming from a distant fan and I look at the smoke puff from my mouth. It feels good here. This is a good spot to lay down.

I look at the bear above me, the way he shakes as I turn onto my back. My nose feels cold now, and my toes, but otherwise I'm ok. *Don't fall asleep.* That's what mountaineers tell each other when they get caught in a snow storm. *Don't fall asleep*, they repeat to each other, over and over again, and they rub each other's fingers and toes and lay close together. But for me, sleep has never felt as tempting as right now. It's so close, right there on the other side. I just have to close my eyes and I will sink into the warm pool. But I'll let it come when it does. In due time it will come.

Everything is cold now. My back, my legs, my face, everything except my head. The trick, I've figured out, is to close your eyes. As soon as you close your eyes it becomes warm. The nicest of warm. I open one eye and keep the other eye closed, then I switch sides and almost start laughing. Now half my body is warm and the other half is cold! But the air is very hard and I can't pull it in deep enough to laugh.

Mr. Bear has come alive. I feel blood moving through his veins; it's boiling forward and I feel his pulse. I really do feel sorry for him. What a crummy destiny. Alive but caught in a body that won't move.

Frozen in time. This is where it ends for him, in a freezer in Manhattan. Him and me. This is where it ends for both of us. Did I turn off the stove? Did I hand in the keys? I guess it doesn't matter. I could sleep for a lifetime.

Yes, you go to sleep little one. Daddy will sing you a lullaby.

I try to open my eyes but a voice commands me not to. It's not an angry voice at all; in fact, it's very soothing.

Go on, close your eyes and sink into the warmth.

Even the tapping is as gentle as a caress and it dances slowly over me. Tap-tap, tappety-tap, tiny fingers probing my body.

Let it go, sink deeper and deeper, come into my arms, my son.

I hear a father. I don't think it's my father but he definitely sounds like a father. Tap-tap, tappety-tap, all over my body.

Oh no, now the voice is angry with me.

How dare you! Don't you touch him!

It rumbles from behind the clouds but I can't see him. I think it might be God. Yes, of course it is. It's definitely God.

Her face is really close to mine. I feel her breath against my cheeks and she's holding my hands between hers.

Charlie, I say, but she doesn't answer.

She only keeps breathing hard, all over my face. She touches my body, rubs my back and pushes me around, saving me all over again.

No, I moan.

If she could only let me be for five more minutes; I don't want to move just yet. But she doesn't listen and keeps pushing me around until I finally open my eyes. I've come to a place where everything hurts. My eyelids, my face, my lungs, my entire body.

No, I say, because it seems to be all I can say, hoping she will go away.

She keeps on pushing me, again and again, and I feel myself rolling around on the platform. I look up and see the bear far above, only to realize that it's smiling at me.

You bastard! This time actual words come out of my mouth. Then I see the Japanese woman.

Somehow she is here too. She leans over me and holds her hands on my cheeks, but something must be terribly wrong with her, because her hands are on fire. She helps me up to a sitting position and I look around but I can't see Charlie anywhere.

Shhh, she says and holds one finger in front of her lips. She keeps kneading and pushing me where I sit until I get a prickly feeling in my arms and legs that makes me want to move. I grab hold of her with one hand and put my other hand on the bear and push away from the platform. Everything spins and flashes but after a few seconds I'm alright. We walk back to the steel door close together, I am leaning on her, and her hands never stop rubbing me wherever they can.

I'm ok, I say as we walk, and when we get to the street I tell her again,

I'm ok.

I even make the sign with my hand.

She looks deserted where she stands on the sidewalk. I watch her through the window in the back and I don't know if it's love or hate I feel.

18

T he elevator is hot and I start sweating as soon as I step inside. Something must be wrong with the heating because it's the same in my room. I think about calling down to the lobby to see what's wrong but I'm too tired and instead I open the window to let some air in. Sweat is pouring down my back and before I do anything I get out of my clothes and take a cool shower. Afterwards I feel a lot better and even though it's still pretty early I close the window and go to bed.

It's the middle of the night when I wake up to a sharp hacking sound. At first I think it's someone knocking on the floor above me. Someone is relentlessly banging the floorboards with their heels, creating a short, chopping noise that bounces off the walls and rattles my bed, but as I try to sit up I hear it's my own coughing. I say 'try' because I really can't. Something is holding me down and I feel that painful hacking inside my head every time I cough.

The next time I wake up I see that the light on the desk has been turned on. I still can't sit up and I sure as hell can't remember getting up to turn the light on. The only thing I can really move is my head but I can only lift it a few inches. Trouble moving my body isn't the only thing that's wrong; something has happened to my pillow, and the entire bed as well. It's completely soaked in water. Every time my chest heaves and my head turns to the side I feel that everything under the cover is completely soaked. And the room, the room is no longer warm but icy cold. Colder even than the freezer. I shake and I feel the wetness all around me and in the fog between my eyelashes I see the honey golden bulb from the lighthouse visible through the foaming storm in the distance, even though I know it's just my desk.

When I wake up again it has started to snow. Some of it has fallen directly into my room and has landed on the carpet. There's a small pile of it behind the chair. My jaw hurts terribly and I can't open my mouth, and every few seconds I have to tighten all my muscles to keep the shaking from going out of control. My face is wet from the beads of sweat that break loose and race down my forehead and tumble off my chin. I blink once and I'm no longer in the Roosevelt but in a hot and sticky jungle. The print on the wall has come alive and the leaves are deeply green and sway from side to side in long hypnotic movements. I watch them as I feel the fever race through my veins.

When I wake up again my teeth hurt. I'm tied to a raft and I can't move anything except my eyeballs, and my teeth hurt like madness. I look down the length of my nose and I see my son sitting on another raft. Both of us are floating aimlessly atop a breathing ocean, up and down. He's sitting with his legs crossed and he's wearing clothes from when he was little. The shirt is the one with the tiny race cars that speed across his chest, but it looks way too small for him now, the way his shoulders bulges out from underneath.

I try to speak; I try to say, *Hey, son*, but my mouth won't open.

It's not dramatic at all. He just looks at me and says,

Hi, Dad, without even opening his mouth.

All around us the sea is moving but I can't actually see the water. I try once more to lift my head but then the coughing starts again.

You don't need to speak, Dad, he says. I can hear you just fine.

There's an aura around his hair; it's all orange, and it makes his head look bigger than I remember it. I lift my pinky finger and wave it at him, and he wiggles his pinky finger back. Then some sort of mist blows in and covers the distance between us and all I can see of him is his contour in the golden light. I close my eyes for a second and when I open them again both my son and his raft are gone.

I don't want to fall into another dream and I fight back with everything I've got. There are stars in my room and they are spinning fast. I try and focus my eyes on them when something stings me and it hurts so much I start to cry. My entire body shaking, I grab onto the board in front of me so I won't fall and through the tears I see that the stars have turned into streetlights. I'm really only standing by the window, leaning on the ledge, with every muscle twitching and sweat dripping from my body. On my knees it doesn't shake so much and I crawl towards the bed and pull the cover down on the floor and roll up in a ball. The vein on the side of my head is the size of a snake.

It's me and him. I know where we are. We've been here before. We've been to this campsite before. It's been a long summer and it's soon coming to an end. I don't know who the other people are; it's just supposed to be him and me. I suppose we can't have the entire Berkshire mountains to ourselves, but those people, why are they here? It's a woman and two children. I know who they are now, and they don't fit in here. They should all come later. Why are they here now? We want some peace and quiet. That's why we came all this way. We walk across the campsite and back, just to see, and sure enough, every step we take they are right behind us.

In the mornings we take our backpacks from the tent and set out. I carry the water; he's only half as tall as I am. We pick things up along the way and put them in our backpacks. When we get back we will catalogue it all. I pick up a colored stone; he picks up a giant pinecone. We keep walking. On the ground below an enormous fern I see a dead woodpecker.

Look, I say and point.

It tried to peck a hole in a tree that was too big, at least that's our theory. We put it in the backpack next to the colored stone and the pinecone. Still, they are two steps behind us. They don't dare come any closer. They keep that distance, all the way back to the camp.

We empty our backpacks and catalogue our treasures with short descriptions. I write everything down in the logbook we bought in the bookstore on 52nd Street on a Sunday. When we roast marshmallows they sit on the other side of the fire. They don't roast anything. They just watch us. There's no purpose in them being here. We refuse to talk to them. The summer goes fast this way and it's over too soon. I fall asleep right there by the fire.

I can feel the scent of the pine and the sweetness of burning marshmallows tickle my nose.

I am certainly pleased, yet confused. There is nothing in the papers about this. Going places, stumbling into people, yes, I've realized those things can happen, but this, this is unprecedented. A character getting sick? Who's ever heard about something so ludicrous. But I will not waste my breath on it, I won't. He's not far away now and if I didn't know any better I would have thought what I felt was a slight pain in my heart. But I'm going to blame that on indigestion.

I'm back on the raft and this time my sister Phoebe is also here. She's sitting right next to me, but she's facing the other way. I have the feeling I shouldn't bother her, not right now. A mist has blown in around us but it never comes close enough to touch the raft. It stays on the edge of the darkness. I want to call out – perhaps she hasn't noticed that I'm laying right here – but my mind stops me. Instead it transforms into a laser that cuts through all things and I see clearly. For the first time I see it all clearly.

This place is like a pantry where all the cans and boxes are stacked neatly and everything stands in the right place. I don't have to search to find what I'm looking for in this pantry. I read the labels and it's all there.

Don't go, I call out, but it's too late.

Phoebe is already in the water, slowly drifting away from the raft. This is a place of total honesty, a place where cans you didn't even know you had, cans you didn't even think existed, are standing in the first row. Even cans you've hidden in the very back are here. It's easy to take it all in. It's like reading the results of the New York Yankees. One, two, three, there it is. Phoebe drifts farther away, not too far for me to get her if I go now, but soon it will be. Still she hasn't turned to look at me. Her hair is long and gray and it floats on the water for a moment before it gets soaked and starts sinking. The feeling that I shouldn't disturb her is still there. I go to the place in the hollow just below my heart and I read the labels. A horn toots in the distance, a lonely and hollow toot. Then the mist blows in and sweeps over Phoebe, and the last I see of her is her hair, gathered like seaweed around her head.

The door to the pantry suddenly slams shut and I am pulled backwards and fall into a black hole. It's the blackest of black and the deepest of holes. It's black the way raw oil is black and it seeps into my eyes and my ears and pulls me down. I think my eyes are open, I probe them with my fingers, but I can't see a thing. All I see is the deepest of darkness and I feel the dull sensation of my fingers pressing against my wet eyeballs.

It's light outside. That's the first thing I notice when I wake up. It's strange really, I'm laying on my back and I open my eyes, wham, just like that, and I notice the light outside. My mouth is so dry I can't even swallow; everything in there is sticking together in one big lump. I don't move, I don't even try. I feel like I'm on the ground after a big fall and now I don't know if I can move my body or if I'm paralyzed. I wiggle my fingers slowly but that's it for now.

Something is different about this morning, something definitely feels different. An angelic stillness lays spread over everything in the room. It's the kind of stillness that comes only after a battle, and it stays only a short time, but right now, this special stillness is here. From the belly of the whale I've been spat out. I've made it through.

The luminous bubble on the wall is gone, but the light on the desk is still on. I feel I'm very close to something, I'm so close I can see the outside of the gate, but I'm not quite there yet. My cough is almost completely gone. I draw a deep breath and it's only way at the end that it breaks down. Was it all in my head or did someone hammer a typewriter furiously last night? I take another deep breath and I sit up. I sit with my feet gracing the very tips of the carpet and there's no flash from the sky, only my dry mouth. Most of my thoughts have left me; at least for the moment it seems as if there's stillness also in my head. I try my legs and stand up carefully. There's no dizziness. I take one step at a time, they feel alright. They feel good. I feel good. Nothing is obstructing the flow in my body. There are no dividers; all the walls are torn. It has become one wide open space.

I walk to the shower and the sensation of the carpet under my feet is phenomenal. It tickles and scratches at the same time. When I look back at my bed I see that it's one rumpled mess. The sheets have been pulled away, revealing the mattress underneath, and the cover is wrinkled and squeezed into a compact ball. It's a battleground and it's taken me so close I can almost reach out and touch it. I have to find a way through. I just know there's something there waiting for me when I do.

I turn the knob and let the hot water rinse off the residue from my fever. Steam rises from all around me and I close my eyes and let the water plaster my hair to my forehead. Seconds turn to stone when my thoughts suddenly come back. Water, seaweed, darkness. The knob is turned all the way to the end but the water still chills my spine. There are things I need to do, places I have to go.

What a schmuck! Why can't he just lay down and die? I ask of him one simple thing, the only right thing, to crawl back into the pen he came from. But what does he do? He get's a fever he's not supposed to be able to get, almost dies from it, then pulls through.

He's had more time than he could ever ask for, creating an entire life out of those 5 days. But why am I even trying? It seems the harder I try, the harder something on the other side pushes back. Sometimes it feels like I have to fight the city itself, as if it's holding him behind his back, protecting him. There's something about that world I just can't get to. Please, don't make me laugh by telling me it's God; my back hurts too much for laughing right now. I'm his God. I'm the only God there is for him. But there is something, there sure is, even though it's not God; there is something working against me and my struggle. I can't really blame him; he doesn't even know what's going on. He's merely a puppet on a string. But this farce could go on forever and I will die before he manages to get things right. I have to take matters into my own hands. That's the only way to get things done. Whatever world you are in, you have to do it yourself. That's the only way. I am the cat and I'll simply wait for him to mouse his way up here.

19

I'm dressed only in my underwear when I hear a knock on the door, and the very next moment it opens up. A short, stocky lady with her black hair tightly spun in a bun walks backwards into the room, pulling along a cart of towels. I stand completely still as the door slams shut, and when she turns around and sees me she is startled. She puts one hand up and holds it in front of her eyes and turns around quickly.

Oh, sorry, sir. They say you no here. Is after 12.

I don't say anything. I had no idea. I'm not

even sure what day it is. I take my pants from the pile on the floor and continue to get dressed.

I come back, she says as she moves towards the door, still with her hand in front of her face.

I try to hurry because I really want to get my pants on before I say anything but my foot gets stuck in one leg and I end up hopping around on one leg, almost crashing to the goddamned floor before I get it right.

No, please stay, I say. I was just leaving.

I look at her where she stands with her back towards me. Her body is shaped like an avocado, round and dark, but in a way that suits her. If I had to guess I'd say she was in her 50´s.

I've been sick, I say. But I'm better now.

My pants are finally on and as I button my shirt she turns around and looks at me for the first time. She looks at my pants, then at my shirt and then finally my face.

You come back? she asks.

I'm not sure what she means, so I say,

Please, stay. No problemo.

She shrugs and pulls her cart across the room and starts with the bathroom. I finish getting dressed and before I leave I watch her work for a little while. She's very fast and efficient. She moves from the bathroom and straightens up things without never really stopping. Everywhere she goes, in front of her there's a mess, but when she has walked by with her magic wand, all the things scatter and rustle to their right place. When she gets to the desk and pulls the cord to the light, I feel my time in this room is over. I'm part of the old dust being swept out to make room for newer things and I know I will never come back. Some things you just know.

The last thing I do is pick up my hat from the floor by the door, turn around and nod a goodbye to the cleaning lady.

Thank you, I say.

But I don't get very far. Halfway to the elevator I hear her shouting from inside the room.

Mr., wait!

She flies through the door as if she's got fire in her ass but immediately slows down when she sees me standing there. Her breath is heavy and between every word there is a pause where she draws in more air.

Whew, Mr., whew. You forget this. Whew, and she thrusts it in my chest before I even see it's a notebook.

It's a ragged old notebook with frail corners, yellowed by age, and a cover that's completely blank. I let it be pushed into my chest and I take it without even trying to explain it's not mine. I'm just too tired to explain anything right now. Besides, all things come to you for a reason.

In the elevator on the way down I listen to the humming of wheels against wires and I realize that the reason I feel so different is because I'm leaving something behind. I don't know what has been the matter with me these last few days, or why I've been so down and out, so to speak. Because the thing is, and deep inside I've always felt this way, the way I feel now, I never really wanted to kill myself.

I cross the street outside the hotel and enter the deli on the corner. I've all but forgotten about the notebook already, but as I stand in front of the fridge and bend forward to pick up a carton of milk, the notebook falls to the floor. I see it laying in the fluorescent light, almost glowing, and I can't help thinking that there's something odd about it. I bend forward and take a closer look at it, but I don't pick it up. The cover is blank, all but for three letters stenciled in minimal handwriting on the upper right hand corner. I'm guessing it's some sort of initials but I really have no idea who it belongs to. I suppose the easiest thing would be to open the damn thing up and see if there are any further clues inside, or even better, just take it back to the hotel and leave it with them. But there's something about this notebook. It's a feeling I get when I look at it. I pick it up and even though it's not in the fluorescent light anymore there's still a slight glowing sensation to it. I look at the tiny letters, J.D.S., at the way they sort of stand out and sit in the air an inch off the paper, and I decide right then and there not to open it. Instead I put it back in my pocket and step over to the register.

The streets around the bus station are alive with pulsating lights. New York is a toy wound up until the spring breaks and then it just spins and spins and there's no stopping it. Everything is dirty here but sometimes you just want to lick it up, suck on each passing hubcap and gum stained piece of sidewalk, and shower yourself in the warm air shooting out from the underground pipes. That's how I feel right now, standing in the midst of it, trying to pick the right bus.

There's something about this notebook that bothers me and I have this crazy idea that if I get on a bus and go north something good will happen. I don't know how or why, but before I do anything else I need to return this notebook to its owner. I can't even say why it's so important; I just have to do it.

There's a reason for everything in life, things happen and you go along, not knowing, because you can't see the bigger picture. But it doesn't matter because life puts you places you're supposed to be for a reason. And that's exactly what I mean. I think I received this notebook for a reason and the reason is that I have to return it. God knows what's in there. For all I know it could be the cure for cancer. I wouldn't want to mess that up. But the truth is that it doesn't really matter what is inside this notebook. I just know that if Mary were alive she would have been the one who found it, and she would have gone through all kinds of trouble to get it back to whomever it belonged to. She was like that, always seeing a meaning in things that happened, seeing herself as one small piece of the great puzzle.

There are important things I need to do. I need to see Phoebe, and I need to see my son, and I need to tell both that I love them. Nothing else is important anymore; I realize that now. But it all starts with this notebook.

The bus that speaks to me most is the bus to Boston. It ends up being a good choice because it is only half full and I get two full seats to myself. When I step off the bus several hours later, I feel the difference in temperature right away. The air up here is raw and moist, like an open oyster, and it blows right through you. I wait around the station for about 20 minutes or so, to see if I get an idea on where to go next. I feel that I still have farther to go, that this isn't the end of the line, and it turns out I'm right.

As soon as I see it I know it's the right place. It's written in white block letters on the upper front of a bus and the letters stand out just like the letters on the notebook, and I think I couldn't have missed them even if I was blind. **Cornish**. It sounds queer in my mouth, almost like something you eat, but the more I say it the better it fits.

I keep going north and the farther north I go the more the trees bleed. I look through the window as we drive through a slaughterhouse of dead leaves hanging very still and damp from hooks in the ceiling.

The station in Cornish is very small, it has only a one-slot parking lot and a sign over a window of the post office where you can get your ticket. I stand on the curb outside the ticket window and watch as the bus pulls out, and I wait a minute before I move, so I have time to melt into the background and for the town to accept me and get on with life. I think I do a good job of fitting in right away, Cornish seems to be a town full of nothing but old people. I see a group of them in front of the post office and I see them outside the church down the street. Old people drive by on Main Street, going very slowly, sitting way up close to the steering wheel in their big, shiny cars.

I start walking towards the gas station across the street to get a drink. The place is empty but for the old man behind the counter.

You're not from around here, he says when I put a can of coke on his counter.

I look at him to see what kind of statement it really is, but I can't tell. He keeps a straight face that could mean anything.

That's right, I say. I came to deliver something.

As soon as I say it I hear how silly it sounds, like I'm in some goddamned movie and I've been sent here by the big city mob to do a job.

It's a notebook, I add, and I take it out of my pocket for the first time since the deli, just to show him that I'm not kidding.

The man takes it from me and holds it in the air at arm's length before his eyes. He squints at the cover and then quickly hands it back to me and starts ringing me in.

What do you want with that? he grunts and punches the buttons on the cash machine harder than he has to.

I don't bother asking him what he means. Perhaps the owner of the notebook and this man have some sort of feud going on, but I don't want to get involved. I just want to deliver it and then go see about what's important, and I walk outside with my coke without another word.

I follow the main road through town. My legs feel strong and rested and I don't mind walking for a while. From a distance I see the postman's car parked by the side of the road; he's hauling a box up to a house and leaves it on the porch. He comes down the walkway just as I pass his car.

Could you point me in the right direction? I ask him.

I hold up the notebook so he can see the initials. It's not much to go on but somehow I know he will get me there, and I'm right.

Sure thing, he says without thinking twice about it and he takes off his glove to point me towards the way I have to go.

He's young to be a postman, twenty something perhaps, and there's not a hair on his face. He reminds me of when I was that age and the world was an open book. When you believed you could become anything you wanted, even if it was going to the moon or sailing around the world in a teacup.

Following his directions I walk back through town and turn left onto a smaller road. He said I should walk for an eternity on this road and then I would get there, and I thought that was a funny way to put it. It really doesn't seem that bad, but as I walk up the first hill and see the road stretch out in front of me, over another two rising knobs, I see his point. The forest is never far away here. It creeps up right to the side where I'm walking. I bet if the roads and the lawns would stay untouched for a while the trees would move in and take over in no time.

The sky in this place is more a sea of yellow and orange than red, and I spot the white mailbox in the distance, a floating buoy in the midst of all this color. I open the box and bend down to look inside. It's empty. I could put the notebook there and take the next bus out of town and go see Phoebe. I've done what I came here to do. But as soon as I think it a wind blows in from nowhere and tugs at the pages. The notebook flips open and quickly rattles through all the pages, and I know I have to take it the last bit of the way.

I ring the bell and stand motionless outside the screen door. I can see myself in the glass, just the very outline of myself, but it's enough. I think of the time my life was smashed into pieces by a notebook, a time that seems both far away and close, and I hope this time it will be different.

20

*E*very *day since I created him, every day since I pushed him through the uterus of my mind, I have thought of him. Every day for 60 long years he's been there with me, like an invisible shadow, and now he's finally here, outside my door. I feel nervous, I confess, but I'm not ashamed to say it. I do feel nervous. I don't think he will recognize me, I'm almost sure of it, but then what things are really sure?*

The bell has only rung once but I know he will not leave before he has delivered what he came to deliver. I walk slowly across the living room floor. My heart is beating in a way I have never felt it beat before, and I stop for a second to watch the outlines of his body through the glass. My boy. I realize just now that I don't even know what he looks like. Inside of me he has a certain look, but that's the look of a young boy. I wonder what time has done to him. I can see the dark shadow swaying a bit from side to side, just a little, and I watch him for a few more seconds with my hand on the doorknob. What's a few seconds when I've waited so long.

I smell the pipe before he even opens the door, but as he does, I can't see that he's holding one. He must have just put it down.

Mr. Salinger, I say.

I can't seem to continue from there.

He looks me square in the face and really stares at me, like I just woke him up or something, but only for a few seconds, then he waves me inside with a flick of his hand and turns his back to me. I have no choice but to follow him. Already I have forgotten what his face looks like. From behind I notice he was once a tall man but now he walks hunched over, resembling a letter C that isn't quite bent properly.

I look at his back as he shuffles through the room and my eyes follow along after him, towards a corridor on the other side. There's hardly any furniture in this first room, only a sofa and an old piano that doesn't seem to ever be played as the keys are all covered in a layer of dust. I only really want to explain how I found this notebook, hand it over and be on my way, but I can't very well just stand outside the front door all alone, so I have no choice but to follow him.

The house didn't look very big from the outside but we walk through so many rooms and hallways before we finally stop that I get confused. We've made it into what looks like a study and he goes directly over and takes a seat in a swivel chair in front of a desk, without asking me if I care to sit. He must also wonder why I'm here, although I have to say, he doesn't show it at all. I'm beginning to think that perhaps he has me confused with someone else. That happens more often than you think for people after a certain age.

I look around the room and I see shelves lining all the walls, except one, and all of them are stacked high with piles of books. When I take a closer look I see that most of them are notebooks, thousands of them, many exactly like the one I'm still holding in my hand. Finally, he invites me to sit and points to a chair behind me. I sit down and as I do I look directly into the painting on the wall behind him. It's strange really but I don't want to look directly at him while he is looking at me. I mean, I'm not afraid of him, but my face is more comfortable looking at the painting behind him than meeting his eyes. I'm guessing it's from India because it has that oriental look to it. A woman with blue skin and a veil you can see through sits in a boat, and on the shore there are men and a herd of sheep. I don't know if they want to get on the boat or if they have pushed it away from shore, and just as I'm about to ask about it, he turns his gaze from me and starts typing.

He sits hunched over an old typewriter and his fingers flow smoothly over the keys. He's caressing them more than punching them, but the sound is still sharp and fast. Without looking up from the paper he says,

I've been waiting for this.

Suddenly I feel myself getting up from the chair to go and stand in the middle of the room, right on a spot where the wood is slightly darker than the rest. I can look at him now without any problem and I see that he must be older than me, probably closer to 90. I glance down at his desk and next to the typewriter is a pile of paper stacked high, weighed down by a heavy cast iron dog.

I've waited a very long time.

He mouths the words slowly and articulates each syllable, as if he is speaking to an empty room. Then he lifts his hand and types the last key with his hand coming down from high above, doing a giant dive, the way a piano player ends a long piece.

He turns towards me on his swivel chair and it's only first now that I get a good look at him. He looks a lot like the average old man I would say, with gray hair, shriveled skin and dried up bones. I've seen it so many times before that it's hard for me to tell them apart. Much like looking at one newborn baby after another. But there's something different about him, something I haven't seen exactly the same before, and it's his eyes. His eyes are dark and deep and almond shaped. They are the only things in his face that seem not to have aged. They are still as deep as I imagine they were since the time when he first opened his eyes. I feel his gaze on me where I stand. It's sharp and bullet like and it pierces me when he speaks.

You couldn't possibly know, he says.

I wait for the rest to come but it never does.

I should get going, I say.

Right after I say that he starts laughing. He starts laughing real hard, banging his knee, over and over again. He even rolls the chair out a few feet from the desk so he can bang it better. The room fills with his roar and from the violent way in which he's laughing, I'm afraid he will fall down dead any second. I want to leave but yet I just stand here on the dark brown spot, unable to move. Eventually his laughter is silenced but it doesn't die out completely.

He still chuckles between the words as he speaks.

I know, he says, don't I know it.

As soon as his laughter has subsided completely, and all I hear is his heavy breathing that soon softens too, the room once again fills with silence. He keeps his eyes locked on me the way a painter takes a step back and looks at his canvas in between brush strokes. I look back at him now, but as I do there's still that felling inside me that I shouldn't. But I do it anyway.

We are watching each other from across the room and it's so quiet I can't even hear my own heart beat.

I need to ask you a small favor, he says.

Even before I can answer I know I will do it. I will do anything he asks me to do.

He turns around perfectly and walks over to the filing cabinet without hesitation. He's become so old, just like me. But we're not the same. No, we are not equal in any way. I am real and he is only a fantasy. A fantasy that tore loose and abandoned the flock maybe, but still a fantasy. He bends forward, not as an old man, but straight from the waist, and I see his pants lift slightly from his ankles. I told him to put it in the green file because the green files are in the bottom drawer.

The dog feels heavy in my hand as I stand up and hold it behind my back. I don't think he will turn around – it's not in my paper – but I don't know for sure.

I hear him stand up but I don't turn around. I should just put the notebook in one of the green files so I can be over and done with this and be on my way, but as I reach forward to do so, something catches my eye. I can't really decipher the information right away; it's too much and too confusing, and on top of that I hear him speak.

You've come a long way.

I hear his voice from behind. I'm reading the tags on each file but still I don't get what they mean. My mind is too occupied with his voice. Why, of course, the man in the gas station. That's how he knows. Word travels fast in a small town. The next thing I know my mind catches up with me. I don't hear him coming up behind me anymore; I don't hear anything at all anymore. All I can do is read the little tags on each file. They're small printed letters and the letters create words I recognize so very well. Pencey. Mr. Spencer. Stradlater. Phoebe. D.B. Prostitute. Maurice. Museum of Natural History. Rye. Merry-go-round. Even Allie. It's all here. My entire life is here.

Something doesn't feel right. There's a heaviness in the air and my hair is standing on end. I can feel it under my shirt. The dog is heavy in my hands and I'm sweating. I mustn't let it slip. I take another step closer. Once will be enough. He's bending forward but the notebook is still in his hand. He seems to have frozen in that position. Perhaps I've done a better job than I thought. The floorboards squeak, I'm sure he must have heard me. But still he stands as still as ever. Which end should I strike with? I think the back, and I tighten my grip on the head. I'm only two steps from him now. If he turns I will strike him from the front. The last he will see in this make-believe world of his is this dog.

I hear him move closer but I don't move at all. All I can do is look at the little tags. Everything in my head is silent. I don't think I've been this silent inside in my entire life. I'm not confused; it's just that I'm all still inside, like I have turned into stone. Then suddenly I feel myself break in two, then in five and ten and eventually a thousand little pieces. I crack from head to toe as if I have been struck by the sledgehammer of God. But I don't fall down, or even into the filing cabinet over which I'm bending; I only stumble where I stand, a drunkard catching his balance, and then I lift my aching body and stand tall.

I turn around and see him standing right behind me, but I can't see him very well because everything is a blur. Tears have filled my eyes and I'm crying like a baby. Even so, I still notice him standing there, with one arm behind his back.

It wasn't the bottom drawer like I told him. I told him the bottom drawer and not the middle one because I know what's in the middle one. I know and now he knows. The moment my hand was about to swing, I had the dog in a steady grip and I was about to bring it down,

I saw it was the wrong drawer. Now I just stand here. I lost my momentum but there's something worse. I can feel it. Something worse is happening.

      I can't make it stop and I cry like a goddamned baby. I don't want to be here, I want to go away. I want to be close to Mary, I want to be with Daniel and with Phoebe, but still I know this is where I belong. I know it so well because I can feel it deep inside, this is where the silence comes from. I just know this is the one place I belong in the world, and that's why I'm crying. I'm crying because I hate this to be the home I longed for my entire life.

      I see him though my tears and I can tell that he knows. He looks so very old the way he turns around and walks over to his desk. The dog looks too heavy for him and he puts it down on the pile of papers with a sigh and turns towards me. At first I think he is about to say something but he doesn't. He just stands there looking at me and before I know what is happening he starts crying too.

     Something is wrong. Something is terribly wrong. I'm standing here looking at him cry, trying to feel nothing, thinking of getting the dog again, and suddenly I can't breathe. I can't breathe because something is stuck in my throat and my lungs and the only way I can get it out is to cry. So, here I am, the biggest schmuck in the world, crying my eyes out in front of my… I'm right here, crying my eyes out. I don't want to think about it. I don't want to get this word in my head. I'm crying and I try not to think, but I can't help it. There it is, the word that hurts more than any knife in the world. I'm crying my eyes out right in front of my son.

I want to get out of here. Even though I see light shining from the windows down the hall, the air is stale and it feels like I'm in a bunker. But I can't move my body, not even an inch. I open my hand and the notebook falls to the floor and I watch the man in front of me and the tears that roll down his face. The muscles in his face don't move at all; his face is completely relaxed while the tears keep squeezing from the corners of his eyes. I feel I have to be the one; otherwise we will just stand here forever. But I don't know where to begin. I mean, what should I ask? Why is my life in your file? Why is this the only place in the world that my body is silent? Why are you crying?

All these are good questions but all that comes out of my mouth as I begin to speak is,

I found your notebook in my room.

I have never felt before what I'm feeling right now. It sits somewhere in my chest and I can't control it anymore than I can control the flames in a fire. It burns

almost the same and all I can do is endure.

    How beautiful he is. How can I not have noticed this before? His body is made from tiny pieces of ink, piece by piece stacked on each other. How could I not have seen this? I can't do it. I can never in my life do it. The fire burns in my chest and I stand here and take it. It burns because of what I was about to do and I thank any god for that stinging pain, any god who hasn't already turned its back on me.

Suddenly I feel very tired and I sit down on the floor, right where I am. My mind cannot grasp what's happening and I feel it protesting when I try to understand. Just like a motor pushed to the limit, my motor is coughing and black smoke covers my mind. He lifts his hand and I hear him sniffle and blow his nose in something. I'm just so tired I need to rest for a while. The silence inside me is complete and thicker than my own body. It extends all through me and shoots out from my stomach and all around the room. I notice he has moved away from me and is now in his chair again. I hear the typing in a haze that drifts my way, as if the taps can't quite make it all the way through the thick wall of silence.

    I'm setting things right. I've been blinded for so long, and now, finally I'm setting things right. I deserted him. I turned my back on him. I disowned my own son, and now I'm making it right. I can still make it all right. There's still time. There has to be. There's only warmth in my heart for him, there ever only was. That's the truth I have just realized. How could I have been this blind! I couldn't be free of him, even after trying all these years, for one simple reason only. Deep inside I didn't want to.

I know the word for this and I am not afraid to use it. I am ashamed and I am all the things that I deserve, but the one thing I am not anymore is afraid to say it. He is part of me as much as I am part of him and I just want to make it right. Please, dear god, help me this once to make things right. Because you see and hear me, because you know when I speak what I have never before spoken. I love him. I love him.

I hear the clatter of the typewriter, it's right in my ear, and suddenly I'm on my feet again. I'm dizzy and still a bit unsteady, but my bladder is full and I have to use the bathroom. I have to use the bathroom right away and I don't have to worry about how to find it because I enter the corridor and open the first door to the right and there it is.

I listen to the sound of the typewriter as I stand by the bowl and I hear it come to a sudden stop. I stand where I am even after I'm done, my pants are still down and I'm holding my shriveled penis in one hand; the light from outside is enough for me to see in the dark room. I stand there as if I'm waiting for something and I think I can hear someone cry, but I'm not sure.

There are things you can give and there are things you can't. I'm giving him the things you can't give because I'm taking it from myself. I'm taking pieces from myself that I will never get back and I'm giving it to him and I feel it is the right thing to do.

I need to be that knight now. For once in my life it really matters. Paper, ink, thoughts and stories, they are all trivial things, but for once it really matters. This is a question of life and death, and I need to be that knight.

It's not a long way to go but it's a way filled with treacherous holes that if you fall down they lead to places I can't reach. I need to sharpen my lance and be the best I have ever been and I need to do it right now. Up to this point it has been a child's game, a lesson learned in school. Right now, this is for real and I need to be the knight that guards him every step of the way. What I will give is also what I will lose, because I will send him away. Now that I just found him. If I could wish for one thing it would be for him to be here, close to me, forever. But just for that very reason I can not allow it. This is what I will give him, the gift that makes him whole. I will be his knight and I will show him the way home.

I hear the familiar tune of the typewriter start again and I pull my pants up and flush the toilet. I don't even walk back into the room, I start walking up the corridor, away from the tapping sound. I'm not sure about the way, but it turns out I don't have to think about it. All I have to do is walk and soon I'm standing right inside the front door again. I put my hand on the knob and I know in my heart that I will never come back here.

I close my eyes and try to hear the tapping, and I still do. It's there, in the back of my mind, delicately hammering out a steady rhythm. I don't know what just happened, or where I have been. It feels like I fell into a giant bowl of boiling oil and that all was lost, but somehow I managed to crawl over the edge and slide down to the floor, unhurt. I've passed some sort of gate and now the road lies open ahead of me. I know I need to get going; I have stops to make. I take one last check of the silence in my heart and I open the door and step outside.

21

Iwalk past the mailbox, up onto the road, down the three hilly knobs and I make a right and go straight to the bus stop. I don't want to think about what just happened or what it means, if it means anything at all. I just want to get going. One day I will sit down and think about all this. I will go back in my mind and I will think about every little detail, and I will lay the puzzle out piece by piece. But not right now. Right now I have more important things to do.

I'm lucky because a bus pulls in just as I get there and again I get two seats just to myself.

Through a half slumber I watch the glowing torches parade by outside the window until we pick up speed and move so fast everything becomes a colorful blur.

I sleep most of the way back to New York and it's late when we get in. I walk around the terminal all night because I don't feel like getting another hotel room and at five, when the coffee shop opens, I still have four hours left to wait. I drink cup after cup of coffee and I run back and forth to the bathroom.

I go outside to get some air. I cross the street and continue for half a block to kill some time. There aren't many people out at this early hour. The sun is up but it's still too low to reach above the buildings. Instead it divides itself into millions of glittering pieces and finds its way through the side streets, all the way from the water. I pass a bookstore and pasted against the window is a map of Manhattan. Just for fun I stop and put my finger right on the spot where I am now. This place is just something. So many secrets behind so many brick walls. But she is beautiful. I slide my finger across the glass, across the map, from the bus station, up to the park, to our old place, back to the park, tracing the way I have walked these last days. My finger seems to remember every step I've taken. It keeps moving through the streets, down to Chinatown, to Union Square, back to the Roosevelt several times, all around Manhattan, until it ends right back where I'm standing right now. I have history at my fingertips, my life in a shop window. I trace it the other way and move my finger backwards, retracing each step I've taken. I go back and forth like this, flowing between present and past, present and past, until it's time for me to get on the bus.

I get my ticket and head downstairs. This bus is completely full and I try not to take up too much space and I stick my hands in my armpits and fall asleep against the window, thinking of Phoebe. Sometimes, but not very often, I let old tapes play of her. Strange though, how she seems closer to me right now than she has these last 60 years.

We arrive in Philadelphia just before lunch and it's a nice day with a blue sky and everything. At first, when I get off the bus and walk through the station, I feel alright about the whole thing, and I go straight to the bathroom and empty my bladder. But then all of a sudden I become nervous. I'm not tired or hungry or anything, only nervous. I splash some cold water in my face and try to breathe it away. I count all the white tiles I see in the mirror behind my back, and that takes away some of it.

I go and take a seat on a bench across from my gate and on my way over there I almost trip over a dog lying on the floor. It belongs to a young girl; she can't be more than 7 or 8, and she's holding on tight to its leash.

Come, Creampuff, she says and yanks the

leash towards her to get the dog out of my way.

It's just the kind of dog you'd expect a 7-year-old to have. A small, white fluffy thing, so fluffy that you can't really tell one end from the other. Her mother is sitting right next to her, reading a book, and she has a bunch of bags around her feet. In fact, she has so many bags that if she were footless I wouldn't have been able to tell.

I don't speak to anyone, even though when I'm nervous I could talk to a plant about the weather if I had to. Instead I get up and get a sandwich from the cart by the newspaper stand; then I go back to my seat. I eat my sandwich and watch the girl pull on Creampuff's leash until the dog gets tired of being pulled on and sinks to the floor with a sigh, and refuses to move. Soon, a rusty metallic voice calls my bus over the loudspeakers, echoing throughout the hall. The little girl takes Creampuff in her arms and as her mother picks up all the bags I see that she really does have two feet, and I walk behind them to the bus. This was once Phoebe. This was once every little girl, I think, and I take a seat close to them.

It only takes 40 minutes for my stop to come up, and as I pass the little girl on my left I smile at her and the dog.

Goodbye, Creampuff, I say and smile.

The girl looks surprised and squeezes Creampuff tighter in her arms, just in case I might try to steal her dog.

I stand motionless by the side of the road until the bus leaves. The bus engine roars when it pulls away, revealing a sign behind its shiny hull. Strawberry Hill, it reads, and I cross the road and start walking up the driveway.

I think they must build them from the same plan because the driveway is, if possible, even smoother than the one at Sunnyside. The house looks a lot like Sunnyside as well, except for the sign shaped like a strawberry that hangs outside the front door. In the reception area it's cool and quiet. Perhaps they research what they think old people like: – a really smooth driveway, a pond for fish in the back, and a young girl in the reception area – and they make one blueprint and build them all from that. Sort of like a McDonald's except with people instead of burgers.

The girl is hardly visible from my side of the counter and I try to look as if I belong in the place as I go up to her.

Hello there, I say.

She looks up from the book she's reading.

Hi, she says.

I'm suddenly caught a bit off guard because I haven't really planned this through.

Umm... I'm here to see my sister, Phoebe . . . Hardwell, I say and bite my tongue.

I regret lying as soon as I say it, but then it's too late.

The girl doesn't pick up on the name though.

She only says,

Sorry, but visiting hours are over. You can come back between 10 and 12 tomorrow, and she doesn't even wait for my reply before she nods her head down into the book again.

I guess I could tell her how I've come all this way, and how it's really taken me a long time, and what I've gone through to get here, but I don't feel like arguing. I try not to feel annoyed as I walk past the strawberry sign again and down the unbelievably smooth driveway. I'm a dry piece of wood without thoughts, pouring down a river. I go once behind the electric circuit box to relieve myself, but apart from that I just stand by the side of the road and wait. The bus comes after an hour and when I get on I immediately look for Creampuff, even though I know I shouldn't. That was another bus. Another life altogether. I try not to feel it because I know I shouldn't, but I feel relieved.

His life is now so long gone it's moving by its own momentum. The map is so wide it's impossible to control every part of the story, or to see what's behind the next corner. What I've put in is still there somewhere, growing without any need to be tended to, but the garden has become so big I can't find anything I'm looking for. I try to find the right buttons to press, the right order in which to turn the keys, so when the sun shines on the sixth pillar the ground will shake and the wall will open up.

They need to reunite or he will never be whole. One thing leads to the next and this is a hole he needs to mend before he can go on. I mustn't let him down. I'll keep trying.

It's after 4 when I get back to the station. My head feels sort of light and I think it's because I've been up and about so much these last days. Even so, I don't feel like sitting down again and I begin walking around the terminal to try and shake the fog within me. Part of me wants to do nothing but lay down on soft white sheets and let the smell of detergent carry me away. To just lay there and forget everything. There would be a slight fuzz at first if I came back, but it would quickly go back to normal again. It seems I've been on my way all my life, and now I'm tired of it. Perhaps they haven't even called Daniel yet and to Phoebe it wouldn't make a difference.

I actually feel so tired right now I could lay down and sleep right here on the floor of the bus terminal. Instinctively I reach my hand out and grab the closest thing I find and before I know what is happening the whole damned wall comes crashing over me.

When I open my eyes I see people gathered around me in a circle. A man is on his knees next to me, his head leaning across my chest. I think he must be a bus driver because all I see is his hat. The top few buttons of my shirt have been unbuttoned and another person is waving a magazine in front of my face. It takes a moment for my eyes to regain focus and when they do I lift my head and just like that the crowd scatters. The bus driver lifts his ear from my chest and I see magazines covering my body from my stomach and down over my legs. I remember thinking that that's a strange thing to do, to cover someone up in magazines, but then I see the fallen newspaper stand. I get up on my elbows.

You alright? the bus driver asks.

I try to feel if anything is broken or if anything hurts, but I feel alright.

I just had surgery, I say and magazines slide off my body. A new pacemaker. I guess they didn't tune it properly.

The bus driver looks down at my chest but my fingers are already buttoning my shirt up.

That's where I'm heading now actually, to get it tuned, I add.

I'm ready to feel pain shooting through my body as the bus driver helps me to my feet, but nothing happens. A girl starts picking up the magazines, one by one, and places them back in the stand.

The driver still has one arm on mine, as if he's not sure that I can stand on my own, and he says,

You shouldn't be out walking like that with a messed up pacemaker.

I don't really know why I lie, it's been that way all my life. I lie about the silliest things in the world, and once I start there's no stopping.

They'll meet me when I get off the bus, I say.

He leads me to the right gate and talks to the driver, who lets me on before anyone else, and I thank him and watch him wobble down the steps and turn his broad shoulders to get through the door. Soon thereafter the bus fills up quickly with passengers carrying all sorts of bags and boxes that they cram into the compartments overhead. I feel a bit shaky still, until we hit the expressway, then I'm fine again.

I don't think about where we're going, I just assume it's back to New York, but sitting on the right hand side I can see the sign from far away. Strawberry Hill. He must have mixed up my tickets when he helped me to the gate.

I make my way up the driveway once again, this time a bit faster, and luckily it's not the same girl; this one has a great big mole on her right cheek.

Forgot my wallet in Mrs. Hardington's room, I say before she even gets a chance to open her mouth, and I walk by without slowing down.

The entire place is very still and silent and I haven't seen anyone yet but the girl. I pass a couple of doors but they are all blank, without names, and I don't know what it is I should be looking for. I walk through a corridor and along the wall stand pots of flowers, and above them hang pictures of cats, balloons, waves and flowers, all things you really start to love after you hit 60.

I pass another set of doors and I figure I'd better just start somewhere and check them all until I find her. I press my ear against the first one and wait a couple of seconds. Since I can't hear anything from inside I try the handle and the door pushes open and I step inside.

For a moment the light in the corridor wells in and illuminates a hallway, and before the door closes completely behind me I get a glimpse of a living room. Completely blind, I feel my way along the wall, my hands moving in circular motions in search of a light switch, and when I get to the end of the wall I accidentally knock something down. The crash is very loud and I freeze, expecting an alarm to go off and guards to come storming through the door any second. I listen hard for any sounds but after a couple of minutes I relax and keep looking for the switch until I find it right by the goddamned door.

I see now that what I knocked down was a framed photo. I pick it up and carefully brush the last pieces of glass off. It's a picture of a man and a woman standing in front of some sort of exotic flower. It's a gigantic flower and it towers tall and big behind them. It's so big it seems as if the second after the picture was taken a jagged-toothed mouth opened up in the middle of the petals, picking up the kicking man by his head. The man is sporting a moustache and has struck a pose that could well have belonged to a modern day Hemingway, the way he looks to be leaning on an imaginary rifle after a successful safari. The woman beside him is his lion. Her face is round and sweet but without distinction. She's the kind of person that would be nearly impossible to describe in a witness confrontation. She just has one of those faces that would get away with murder.

Suddenly I hear sounds coming from the corridor and I hurry to flip the light off and quickly step into the bathroom. Just as I close the door behind me I hear the flip of the light switch again, and seconds later a voice that grunts

What the hell? and then everything becomes quiet.

I give in to the situation and let it sweep me away. There's no way out so I drop everything inside and simply sit on the toilet and wait for the strip of light under the door to grow into an entire room. The photo in the broken frame is still in my hand and I listen to the sounds coming from outside. There is the shuffling of feet against the floor, a radio is turned on in another room, then a door opens and closes. I hear the sweeping sound of a broom, then a shrill rumble of broken glass sliding into a wastebasket, then a door opening and closing again. I sit completely still and listen to all these sounds, but after the sweeping and shrill of glass everything is silent.

Then, in one sudden movement the door is pulled open and a very bright light beams over me and for a few seconds I can't see a thing.

I was waiting for you to come out, a voice says behind the blinding light.

I blink my eyes a couple of times and swallow before I see the man in the picture standing there, holding onto the end of my scarf.

You know, he says, you shouldn't leave traces like this behind when you're breaking into someone's home, and he holds it up for me to see.

I pull on my end and as it slides out of his hand I reel it in.

I was looking for my sister's room and I made a wrong turn, I say.

His eyes shift towards the picture in my hand, but he doesn't say anything; he simply turns around.

I have put some coffee on in the kitchen, he says, already on his way there.

When I sit down at the kitchen table I realize I'm still holding the picture in my hand and I lean it against a ceramic angel so it faces his way. Two cups have been placed in the middle of the table, filled to the brim with coffee as black as tar. He pushes one cup towards me and picks the other one up himself. It looks too hot to drink so I don't even try.

I don't say anything and neither does he. He guns his coffee down like it is a glass of water and then, as on key, we both start talking at the same time.

I'm sorry, I say.

You know, he starts, and then there's more silence.

I wait a little while to see if he's about to go again, then I continue.

The picture, I say and nod towards it, I'm sorry about the picture.

He doesn't seem to even notice it and just starts from where he was interrupted.

You know, I don't get much company here, so when I saw the broken glass and your scarf I went directly to the kitchen to put some coffee on.

I wait for words to come into my mind, any words, and what I get is,

Are you a hunter?

He smiles and shakes his head.

No, no, I wouldn't have the heart to shoot anything. His eyes become dreamy. But I was one hell of a shot in the army though.

Just then I think about my mother. She used to say that there was a one-way street between my head and my mouth, and I used to tell her that it was true for everyone, because your mouth *was* in your head, and she would tell me not to be smart.

We talk about life in general, starting in at one end but never getting to the finish. Time flies and my coffee cools down enough for me to drink it, and soon my cup is empty. We both look at the picture and he tells me the woman is his wife; she has been dead for two years. The picture was taken in Hawaii a year before she passed.

I was tired of eating out of a can, he says as his eyes sweeps over the kitchen.

I feel I'm running out of time and I stand up. I look him square in the face and search it for anything I don't want to see there.

I need to find my sister, I say.

At first he doesn't say anything and his face remains calm. Then after a moment of nothing he blinks and says,

You've come to take her away, haven't you?

I don't answer him because it's not until he says it that I know that this is what I have to do.

You've got that face, you know, he says, the face of a man on a mission.

Besides, he continues, visiting hours are over, and his face finally cracks into a smile.

Phoebe's room is in another hallway and I would have spent days looking for her had I stuck with my original plan of trying all the doors. We walk around in a semicircle, across to the other wing, to avoid the reception area.

Well, here it is, he says as we stop outside a door exactly the same as all the others.

You want me to just run in and grab her?

Excitement shines in his eyes and I figure this is probably the best damn thing that has happened to him in years.

I put my hand on his shoulder and I feel that he is breathing hard, as if he is on some goddamned mission in Burma, and I try to sound as calm as I can when I speak.

Wait here and keep an eye out, and before he can argue I open the door and disappear inside.

The moment I'm in and I have closed the door behind me, I see her. It's strange really, not at all as I expected. Nothing falls from the sky and nothing inside me breaks. She's sitting on the edge of the bed with a book laying face down next to her, and it looks as if she was just waiting for me to stop by.

She simply looks up and smiles at me through her glasses, and says,

Oh, hi there, as if I had just popped out to buy a pack of cigarettes five minutes ago.

The door I just opened was a door to the past and what I find on the other side is the same old Phoebe I once left behind. The same girl I used to wake in the middle of the night. The one that used to kill me. Only now she has gray hair.

I feel relieved. I hadn't even noticed I was nervous until now, and I walk up and sit down right next to her and everything really feels alright. Perhaps it's true what they say, that no such thing as time exists between siblings. She takes her glasses off and holds them in her hand. I notice that she's not sitting so straight anymore, not like she used to. There are a million things to tell her but I can't think of any one thing right now. Not any right thing anyway. So, I just let what wants to come out, come out.

Remember when you gave me your Christmas money so I could run away to California?

Phoebe nods her head immediately.

I've done it again, I say. Not the money, I mean, I don't need money, I add. That's not why I'm here.

Phoebe nods again. Words don't even seem necessary between us. Good old Phoebs.

Then she kills me. I mean, she really kills me because her question shoots through the room like a stray bullet.

Do Mom and Dad know?

She looks at me with genuine concern, the same way she used to look when she was little and she saw me smoking or doing some other madcap thing. In a split second those words fill me with sadness.

You know they worry, she continues, about you being kicked out of school and all.

I admit, it's the easiest turn to take, out onto the widest avenue, but I don't know if it's the right way to go.

I won't, I say. I promise I won't be kicked out of school again. Just don't tell Mom and Dad, ok?

A weight falls from her face, and it's a face lined with a thousand tiny canyons. She sighs and acts like suddenly she's the big sister and she was only teasing me all along.

I won't, I promise, she says.

Some white stripes of hair creep out from behind her steely gray hair.

Tell me a story, she says and she scoots over closer to me so that our legs and arms touch.

I notice she still smells like a little girl. Sitting close like this, together we make up 140 years of skin and bone. For a moment I feel the sadness inside me stir and I concentrate on the story. It's the one about the ducks that are surprised by the sudden cold of the winter, and they all freeze to the lake as the water turns to ice. The only way out for them is to fly away with the entire lake stuck to their feet and land someplace warm. So they do, and where it once was a lake became a hollow, and wherever they landed became a lake.

When I'm done I look down at Phoebe and I see that she has closed her eyes.

The door opens slightly and he must be crouching down because all I can see is the top of his head.

How's it going? he whispers and that very scene is so absurd, me here with my sister, about to sneak her out of her home with the help of an old war veteran, that I have to bite my tongue not to start laughing.

Phoebe, I say, get your jacket. We're leaving.

I get up but Phoebe doesn't move and she gives me another worried look.

Mom and Dad are sleeping, I say. They will never find out, I promise. Now lets go.

I'm not sure if I'm doing the right thing. In fact, I don't think I've ever been so unsure, but it's too late to back off now.

We walk through the corridor without making a sound, stopping to look around each corner before we keep going. Somehow it feels more like breaking out of cold war Russia than a retirement home. When we get to the lobby Phoebe and I sneak out behind Hemingway's back, while he occupies the girl by the desk.

He catches up with us as we start down the hill and I can tell he's excited.

We're doing it! he hisses. We're busting out!

An alley of oak trees embrace us from above and he walks ahead of us in a fast pace down the hill. Phoebe brushes up against me and doesn't seem to be bothered anymore. I think it's mostly just that she doesn't know what's going on.

Don't worry. Mom and Dad won't find out, I say, just to make sure.

We stand by the side of the road and wait and as the bus arrives it comes in fast and stops in a small cloud of dust. The door opens with a hiss and I push Phoebe up the stairs ahead of me. Even before he says it I know what's coming. The tap on my shoulder is enough.

I,...I can't, he says and looks at me with big sad eyes.

He takes a step away from the bus and flashes me an embarrassed smile.

It's alright, I say and shake his hand before I get on.

We scramble down the aisle and take a seat so we can wave goodbye to our friend. I see him at the foot of the window, once again leaning against his invisible rifle. As we speed away he becomes smaller and smaller until he is only a speck amongst other specks, moving slowly up the hill, probably for the very last time.

The bus ride is uneventful. Phoebe falls asleep against my shoulder and as I straighten out when we get close to the station in Philadelphia, she wakes up. I notice her earlobes are wrinkled and I picture my sister 60 years ago and I feel my life is a circle, that it's taking me back to the beginning. We move with sleepy steps into the station. It's evening and lots of people stand around waiting for buses to take them places. We sit on a bench and I see the magazine stand behind the pulled down shutters. After a while our bus pulls in, and people well out and hurry off into waiting cars and cabs, and we get on.

We take the two seats in the very front, just to the right of the driver. Phoebe is tired and so am I, but I can't seem to go to sleep even though I want to. It's pitch dark outside and the bus hums and eats the white lines that race towards us with great appetite. I stare at them, one after another, until I finally manage to close my eyes.

Phoebe, I say as I sit up with a jerk and shake her shoulder.

She lifts her head and for a short moment she looks like she doesn't know where she is. Then she lets out a big sigh.

I thought it was all a dream, she says through a yawn that temporarily flattens out her wrinkles.

She sticks her hand under my arm and squeezes herself against me.

I need to talk to you about something important, I say.

I look past her out the side window and I see the reflection of her head, and behind it I see dark shadow figures passing by in a blur.

What is it? she asks, and I'm not really sure where to begin.

I keep watching her, not directly, but the back of her head in the glass, and I feel her eyes on my face the way a blind man's hands would flow over it to feel it's shape and form. The humming of the bus fills the silent space in the background.

I'm sorry, is all I get out before I feel the tears come, and even though I don't continue, I know she has understood everything.

She squeezes my arm tighter and I listen to the humming as she speaks.

You know, he used to call me to talk about this and that and no matter where we started we always seemed to end up on you. I hear my sister's breath moving in and out. He loved you and so do I, she says. I always have.

I don't look at the reflection anymore but now gaze directly at my sister. In her wet eyes I see an old man looking back at me, and right this moment, for a second or perhaps it's minutes, I'm sure I don't know who he really is.

After holding each other the way only a brother and sister can, I sit up and wipe away the last of my tears. I look at her again and I feel sobered up. It's only moments after that I feel it creeping up my spine and I know it's only seconds until it reaches my head.

I need to close my eyes for a second, I hear myself say, and as soon as my head touches Phoebe's shoulder everything goes black.

22

It's late when we get to New York. The blackness around us seems a lot blacker because of all the lights and we get off the bus and wade through pools of neon over to Times Square. I'm looking for a place we can spend the night and we walk directly into the Marriott, which is the first place we come across.

There's something about the porter that seems familiar, but I can't put my finger on it. Phoebe is half asleep, hanging onto my arm while I lead her into the elevator, and the last thing I see as the door glides shut is the vaguely familiar porter.

The key card slides through and as the lock makes a beep I push the door open. Right away I know something is wrong. I see balloons by the windows right in front of us and there's a gigantic ribbon tied across the ceiling. Perhaps they've given us someone else's room. I don't know if Phoebe has noticed anything yet so I elbow her carefully to wake her up. We are standing there, looking into our own hotel room, and the next thing I know a crowd of people jump out from behind the wall, screaming,

Surprise!

They are all there. D.B. is wearing a bowtie and Molly has let her hair out and it floods the entire room. Someone goes round and round on a tricycle and I see that it's Allie. He winks his eye at me and blows a big bubble, without ever slowing down. We step inside and I see Charlie laying on the bed wearing her school uniform, smiling coyly at me. There are friends from the past, even way back from school. The young Stradlater is standing in a corner with a drink in his hand; he smiles at me too and lifts the drink up in a silent salute. Everybody is smiling and wearing silly party hats and some of the multicolored confetti that hangs from the drapes lays strewn around the floor. I take another step and I see my son standing next to his wife and right in front of them are the little girls. It looks like they are posing for a family photo. We walk even farther in and as we do people part before us and in a chair by the window I see Mary. She's just like I remember her. Fresh as a flower. I look up and I read the ribbon. **Happy Birthday**, it says, but I don't know if it's for me or for Mary or someone else. And even though these are all people from my life, I feel out of place.

I wake up as Phoebe shakes my shoulder. The first thing I see is the honey colored fluorescent light in the ceiling outside the window, and I know we're back in New York.

Arm in arm we wade through the pools of neon over to Times Square; all the while Phoebe stays very close to me. We are both ghostly tired and we walk into the first hotel we find, which happens to be the Marriott.

There's a young man behind the counter and from a distance there's nothing out of the ordinary about him. It's Phoebe who notices it first and I feel the grip on my arm tighten. She doesn't even have to say anything because by then I have noticed it myself. The boy behind the counter is an almost exact copy of myself 60 years ago.

I have to wring my arm free because she is hurting me the way her fingers are pushing into my flesh, and I take a good look at myself. I am standing behind the counter at the Marriott in Times Square, wearing a dark blue suit, as if it were the most natural thing in the world.

I step up to the counter and my eyes don't

leave him as I ask to get a room. He only smiles at me and punches the computer behind the desk, and every little hair on him, every movement and every crease, is me. He hands me the key card and my finger touches his for a brief moment and it's my own hand touching myself. I turn around to go to the elevator but I need to check one more thing, so I can be sure, and I go back to the desk.

Can you tell me what time it is? I ask him.

I watch his mouth carefully.

He parts his lips but only to smile, and he points to the clock on the wall.

I try again and this time I ask him,

What time is breakfast served?

He opens a folder and points to the hours under Breakfast and I reach my hands out and get a grip on his suit collar and I pull him closer and I start shaking him back and forth to get him to speak, but still he doesn't say a word and only smiles back at me.

I'm afraid I'm not as steady of hand as I once was. I punch in what I think is right but something else comes out. Having a change of heart, falling over, mixing up the characters – what a mess this has become. I'm trying to find a way out, a clear cut way that leads him straight home, but it seems impossible. I'm too old to fight back like I used to fight. I'm old and tired and all I want to do is sleep.

This world is so much bigger than I first thought and it is no more controllable than any other world. I'm not even sure anymore that they are different places.

I'm down to my last piece of paper. It looks so fresh and white in my hand, so empty and innocent. I take a deep breath and put it in from the top, just like I have so many times before, and with great care I roll it forward to the right position. I rest my fingers on the keys and take a deep breath before I begin. Please don't let me slip.

When I open my eyes I see the honey colored fluorescent light and I know we have arrived at the bus station. Phoebe is shaking my shoulder and I lift my head from hers. The side of my face is wet with saliva and I wipe it off with the outside of my hand. I dreamt something again, but I can't remember what. I just know I dreamt and that I heard the tapping in the background.

We get off the bus and wade through pools of neon over to Times Square. Phoebe is holding my hand and we walk close together, looking for a place to spend the night. We are both very tired and we walk into the first place we find, and it happens to be the Marriott.

The porter hands me the keycard and Phoebe is so tired I almost have to lift her to get her into the elevator. We stand side by side, leaning our tired bodies against each other, and I feel her hair against my lips.

None of this seems real, I whisper.

Phoebe opens her eyes and smiles at me.

I don't even know why I brought you here, I say, and the elevator doors glide open.

Our room is only a couple of steps down the hall and I put my hand on the doorknob, and she puts hers on mine, and for a second we stand like that, looking at each other, as if we are not sure what we will find on the other side. Then, together, we push the handle down and step inside.

When I wake up I see that the sky is a clear blue. Phoebe is already up and she's sitting bent over the desk by the window. I walk over to her and look outside. It really is a nice day; I can't see a single cloud whichever direction I look.

Phoebe is humming softly to herself where she sits. I woke up with the sensation that I've gone through a race of some sort, running through a field full of mines, and I've made it across safely. I go take a shower and call out a good morning to Phoebe from inside. I turn on the water and it drowns out her faint humming. As I get dressed I notice that my suit is starting to look sort of crummy, with heavy wrinkles cutting across the back, and my shirt has a black line along the neck.

You want to get some breakfast? I call out to Phoebe.

I comb my hair and walk over to the desk

to see what she wants to eat. Something inside me breaks every time. I look down and see that the picture she's drawing is of a cat and a flower, and the crayon colors are very bright, and the words Mom and Dad are scribbled over two foamy clouds next to a smiling sun.

My legs feel tired from all the walking I've done lately and I really want to take a taxi, but for some reason I can't find one outside the hotel. I mean, even though we're in the middle of goddamned Times Square I can't find a taxi. So we start walking. It's only about ten blocks or so anyway, so I guess it's alright. The day is crisp, almost newly laundered, and the air is soft and fresh. Phoebe is walking right beside me. She's been acting worried all morning and I keep telling her I will go back to school directly after summer, but it doesn't seem to help. When we cross the street Phoebe takes my hand and I let her. We pass a newsstand on the corner of 50th and I get an urge to stop. It was over 30 years ago but still the same, I can hear Mary and Daniel stomping into the living room, holding onto one side each of the newspaper to show me the latest research, as if it was yesterday.

Wait a minute, I tell Phoebe, and I let go of her hand to go back to buy a pack of cigarettes.

Phoebe keeps quiet and we walk on. I can see the park now, how it spreads out between the buildings up ahead.

You shouldn't smoke, you know, she says, and

her voice has turned into something very delicate and girly. It's not really directed at me, it's more of a statement, and I let it linger in the air until it vaporizes.

The pack feels good in my hand. It seems to remember the shape and feeling of the square box of paper covered in shiny plastic, and I get a sudden urge to light one just so I can please it. I remove the plastic and look through my pockets but I already know I don't have a lighter. Phoebe looks very pleased and I don't even get bothered about not having a lighter because Phoebe is back to smiling again.

I know that somewhere inside her there is a loose wire that you can't see on the outside. It either flows or disconnects but you never know from one moment to the other which of the two it is. As we sit down on a bench, Phoebe immediately starts talking about ice skating and how much fun it would be and perhaps some of her friends are at the rink, and so on. I listen to her speak and watch my breath escape me as an almost invisible white cloud, and I look at the trees around us. I don't know what we're doing here but it feels alright. People on bikes and roller skates pass on the road in front of us, and so do joggers and people walking their dogs. Phoebe dangles her legs and I put the cigarettes in my pocket and stand up. I hold my hand out to her and once again everything is still; only inside me does the ground shake. I feel that my life is just a goddamned story scribbled on a piece of paper and I'm now nearing the end. It feels like I'm on the very last chapter and still I have no idea what to make of anything.

23

I see it appear in a clearing and it all comes back to me at once. We step into the line and there's a glow in Phoebe's eyes and I can feel the same glow in my own. It must be close to lunchtime because baby strollers are parked in a cluster next to us and all the mothers stand below watching their kids go round and round.

It's all the same horses, the same ones they had 60 years ago. I even remember the one Phoebe was on that day I was watching from the ground below, promising to be a better person. Is it possible that's all life is? That space between one carousel ride and the next? I point out the red one and Phoebe gets on it, I take the blue one right next to hers and we don't have to wait long before the world starts spinning. All around us kids are clinging to their horses, smiles on some, fear on others but a light in each of their eyes. Phoebe clings to hers harder than she has to and looks over at me with big round eyes.

Please don't go to California, she says, and she looks at me with a worried face.

I feel my heart stir but before I can even promise her that I won't, that she doesn't have to worry, she throws her head back and starts laughing. Sometimes she really does kill me. I start laughing too and together we spread our arms out and fly across the prairie.

I feel the wind lick the tips of my fingers and the jacket around my waist blows to the side. We spin around and around and the world quickly goes out of focus, but I realize it's only up here where we can really see things clearly. The next thing I know everything goes black.

I'm still here and I lean forward and clutch my horse tightly. Behind the blackness I can hear the music and the air swooshing across the openings of my ears. I feel the carved wood under my fingers, the same wood so many children have grabbed before me. I trace the dried up arteries that spread down the horse's neck with the tips of my fingers and the feeling of the wood fills me up from inside. I hug the horse as tight as I can and even through the darkness I know everything will be alright.

This is the end. I only have a couple of more lines to go after this and I don't know how to fix what needs to be fixed. These last words are for you, my son. I am terribly sorry for everything. Know that I always loved you and that you will always be a part of me, wherever you are and whatever happens to you. I tried my best and I will miss you al...

The first thing I see when I wake up is Phoebe's serious looking face close to mine. I'm still clutching the horse and I breathe right there for a couple of seconds before I sit up. My hands and arms ache and there's a tingling sensation at the base of my back. Through it all, I notice that Phoebe is crying, but without making a single sound.

Don't worry, I say, I'm ok now.

I swing my leg over the horse and stand up just to prove it. As I do Phoebe stops crying but she still looks like she's seen a ghost.

Really, I say, I'm ok.

She whispers when she speaks.

Your pants.

She points discreetly at my pants and

even before I look down I feel the warm wetness between my legs. I've pissed myself again. We hold on to each other as we get off and we walk from the carousel and go stand by the fence.

Don't worry about it, Phoebe says. It happens all the time where I live.

She takes her jacket off and ties it around my waist like an apron. I grab her hand and there's something inside me that I have never felt before. Something is broken and I no longer feel connected to the ground. My sneakers make a sucking sound every step I take, but it's as if my feet aren't touching the ground. We walk past a playground and by the water fountain I see something yellow laying on the ground. It's so perfect because it's the missing lighter and I bend down and pick it up. The pack that was brand new not long ago is now all bent out of shape; I must have crushed it while hugging the horse, but I find one cigarette that's still whole and I pull it out. Phoebe glares at me from the side but she's smiling and doesn't say anything. With a steady hand I light it and draw in the first smoke to enter my lungs in 30 years.

Are you ok? Phoebe asks, but I don't answer her right away.

I squeeze her hand and we keep walking. I take another long drag and fill my lungs to the brim with smoke. Then I flick the cigarette to the ground and let it all out. Through a huge, white cloud of smoke I start laughing.

I look at Phoebe and I can't help but laugh. The last of the smoke shoots from my mouth, right into her face, and I laugh. My piss-filled shoes squeak every step I take and I laugh. Phoebe starts too and together we laugh so hard we have to stop and sit down to catch our breath. I have no idea about anything and that's ok. For the first time, that's ok, and we can't stop laughing.

We hear the screams of children from where we sit, and we can see the playground to our left. Behind us there's a big rock formation that swells up from the ground; it looks like a miniature version of a mountain. To our right the rock ends and the bench we sit on is placed just below the westernmost tip of it. Phoebe's hand feels good in mine and when I lean back and look up I stare right into the overhang that looms over our heads. The surface looks so smooth and familiar, as if we were all made of the same stuff. I pull the air deeply into my lungs. Where we sit the air smells of earth and pine, and right now, even though I'm sitting here in my piss-wet pants, there's not a thing in the world I would like to change

I listen to the kids scream and I watch them run around the playground. Kids are really in a secret world of their own. Both Phoebe and I watch the playground and the miniature people in their colorful clothes, living in a miniature world. Just like squirrels, kids belong in parks.

Straight below us two kids try to climb a tree but it's way too big for them and they only get an inch from the ground before they fall on their backs. I listen to the noise coming from everywhere around, from the playground, from the tree, from up above, and it's all a good sort of noise. I could listen to kids screaming and laughing all day. I close my eyes and picture them running after each other. So much energy. Some of the screaming comes closer, then it moves away, just like a breath. Like the park is one giant lung that lifts us all up and down.

I think about the park, I can actually *feel* the park in my veins. I bet even my blood is green. Suddenly, and without thinking, my legs push the bench away and I find myself standing up. It's not as before, when I did things without knowing why; this is coming from a different place. This is coming from the park. At the very same moment I stand up the screaming is cut off and I open my eyes wide and see something in the corner, a red little dot, and all I have time to do is lift my arms up with my palms facing the sky.

A red bundle lands in my arms with a soft thud. It's a small bundle but it's heavier than a rock, and I fall backwards and roll around on the ground. Wet leaves get plastered to my face and I notice how sweet they smell. Everything is silent and I look at one leaf in particular that is so close to my eye I can see its arteries. I try to breathe but I can't and everything is dead silent. The world is zipped up in a soundproof bag and I feel the good old blackness coming back. Twice in one day, something that never happened before, I manage to think. Something in my chest moves and as the leaf falls from my face a tiny little face looks up at me, he looks more surprised than scared, and before everything becomes black I get a look at his straw blond hair and I see that he only has two big front teeth.

I'm in a field. It's a gray day and only the very tips of the grasses move from side to side with the wind. It's like the ground is breathing. Nothing else is here but me and the field, and I'm standing right in the beginning of it. Before me it spreads out as far as I can see. There's something I have to do. I know because I don't want to. My stomach is tight and I'm afraid. Only when I begin to run do I know that's what I'm supposed to do. The rye is shoulder high and it parts to let me through. Loose pods fall off their stems and stick to my pants and arms, but I don't stop running. The sky is the same gray mass I've seen before, it seems to be all around me. There's only the sky and the rye. Up there the sky, and to either side the golden brown rye.

I lean forward and keep running. I start to sweat and some pods stick to my forehead. I hear the long stalks break under my feet and I hear the wind move through the sun brown vines, almost like a whisper. I know I shall keep running. It's very important and I will know when to stop. The field has a sweet earthy smell and I hear the 'ritsch ratsch' of the rye against my body, and I pump my arms back and forth as my legs go up and down. There's an ending where there's an ending. I will just keep running, I have to.

I'm not tired. I breathe hard and I hear my heart beat but I'm not tired. I keep running. 'Ritsch, ratsch, boom, boom.' I don't look down, only forward and up. All I see is honey golden rye and the gray sky. Then the rye ends.

It's so sudden. One moment it's a wall all around me and the next it's gone. I don't know if I ever stopped running or not. But now it's too late. There's no more field, just wide open space. I'm falling forever, tumbling through empty space and I don't know what's up and what's down. There's only the gray sky but it's whirling past so fast I can't focus. My stomach is sucked in flat against my spine and I keep tumbling through the air, going round and round.

There's a hollow thud when I land. A ringing sensation lives on in my stomach, just like rings on water. My arms are outstretched and my face is old and without any strips of grass sticking to it, and when I look up I see myself holding myself.

24

It's all white here, except for the flowers on the table. The covers are real fluffy too. I figure they wouldn't be any more fluffy even if they were one part cloud and one part cover.

As I lay here I can hear them talking in the corridor, but I can't make out exactly what they're saying. I look at things as they float by; I thumb through the polaroid's of life. Really, it's an entire lifetime of things.

Phoebe is in another room down the hall. She came with me up here and she stayed. She still goes in and out of it, but that's just the way it is. What's important is that we're never leaving each other again. I've been too far away from the people I love for too long. By the way, I say up here because we are in the mountains.

I move my fingers, hands, legs and head. Everything is working just like it should. I sit up and get out of bed and I walk across the floor and open the window. I feel the cool air lick my chest and I go and lay down again. I close my eyes and let the coolness pass through the room until it reaches my nostrils. I smell the air rather than breath it. I could go anywhere on earth but after these few days I will still always be able to tell you if it's mountain air I'm breathing or not. Even with a goddamned blindfold on.

My son is coming today. He's driving up from California to visit his father. I take another deep breath and I get up.

It's a cloud free day. The sky is a bottomless field of light blue and there's a very soft wind blowing. It's usually very still up here, and so it is today as well.

I'm at a table writing this. I've been sitting here now for several hours. The last time I told you about it I was in a place much like this, but this time I'm getting things right.

I don't plan on writing another after this one, so I'd better get it right.

I see him coming through the glass doors and

I get up and stand in a spot in front of the table. I'm not sure if I should move. At first he doesn't notice me. I'm standing very still and the sun is shining in behind me, right into his eyes. The girl smiles and points my way and then I feel it's a good time to start walking. I can't describe what I feel. We reach each other halfway. He's nothing but a big smile and I open my arms and I move forward. I take him in and he lets me. I love him for many reasons but one of the reasons is because of that.

We hold each other this way for a long time. I feel myself warming up from the inside out and I feel my heart as if it's a small animal living deep inside me. Every little piece of me he warms up. My son. It's a hug that makes up for lost time. Don't believe what anyone ever tells you; hugs can fix what you think can never be fixed. Our tears come easily and they are tears without pain.

We step outside into the Japanese garden. We are all alone except for the two carp that swim silently around the pond like dead logs, pushing a small ridge of water ahead of them. We walk across the tiny bridge and sit next to each other on the circular stones. Around us the tall green grass sings in a hushed tone, whispering as we speak. I go first.

I take my son's hand and look him straight in the eyes. I'm through the gate now and I won't ever get lost again. It's so easy once you're through, believe me. There's only one way you can go really.

It's a pretty hard life, you know. Sometimes you end up feeling crummy no matter what, but you can never give in to that crumminess. Never ever.

He has D.B.'s eyes and he looks at me. I feel my son's pulse mix with mine and we're in no hurry to be anywhere else. So, I inhale deeply and take it from the beginning.

Did I ever tell you about the catcher in the rye?